How I Found the Riches of the Christian Life

Dallas Jones

Copyright © 2003 by Dallas Jones

How I Found the Riches of the Christian Life
by Dallas Jones

Printed in the United States of America

Library of Congress Control Number: 2003091983
ISBN 1-591605-63-6

All rights reserved. No part of this publication may be reproduced or transmitted in any form or by any means without written permission of the publisher.

Bible quotations are taken from the Holy Bible, New International Version Copyright © 1973, 1978, 1984 by New York International Bible Society. Used by permission of Zondervan Publishing House. All rights reserved.

Xulon Press
www.XulonPress.com

Xulon Press books are available in bookstores everywhere, and on the Web at www.XulonPress.com.

For Pastor Vernon and JoAnn Morse,
Special, dear friends in Christ who always encouraged me in completing this book.

Dallas LeTourneau

*"I have come that they may have life,
and have it to the full."
(John 10:10)*

For Gretchen

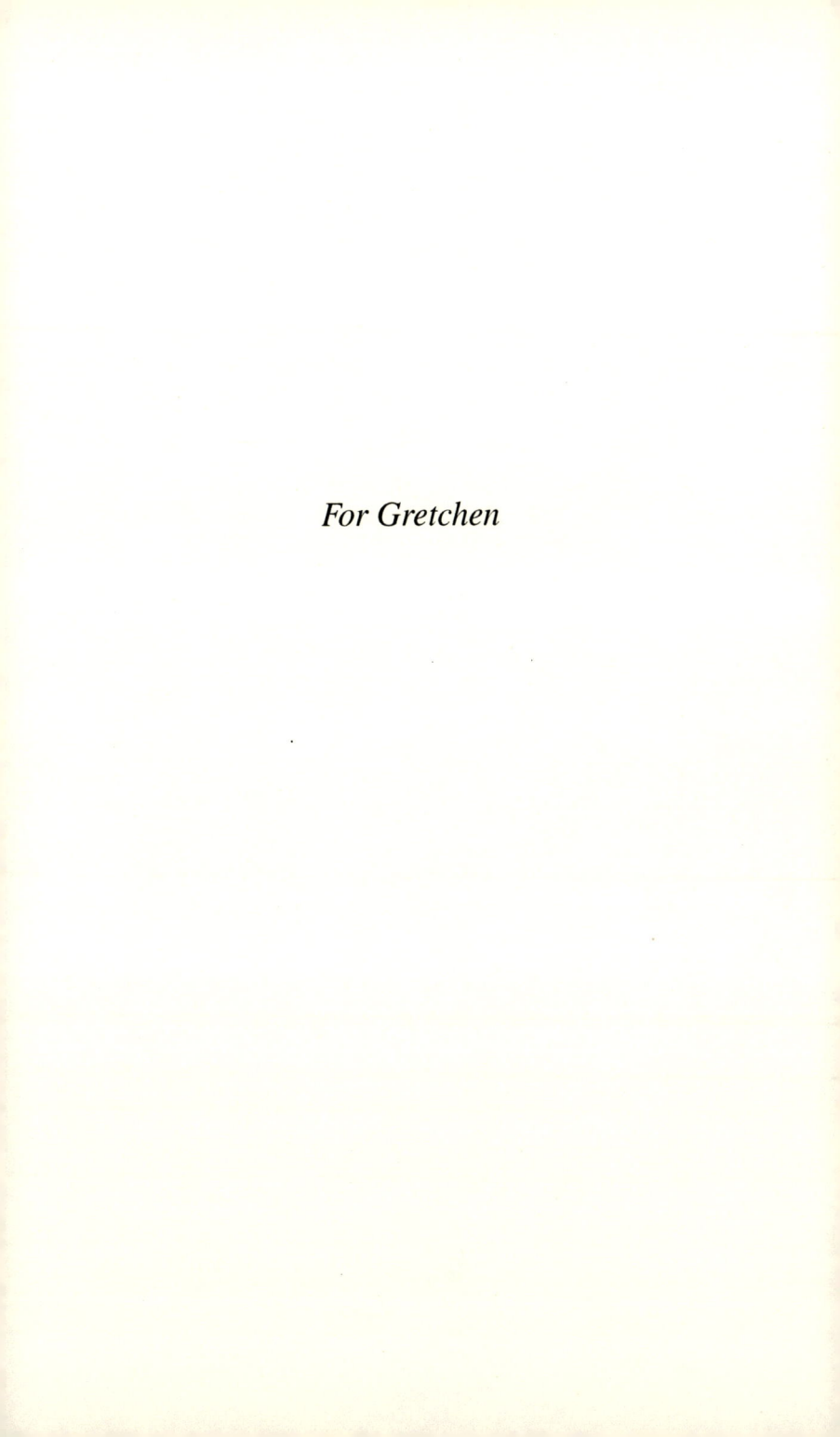

Endorsements

"How I found the Riches of the Christian Life" comes out of the author's spiritual journey from the emptiness of worldly success to a fulfilling life and peace of mind through Jesus Christ. It was my privilege to share personally in a part of the journey. The book includes core truths of the Christian faith. It is Biblically grounded and theologically sound. It will enrich and inspire, give encouragement and insight to all who read it.
—*Lawrence A. (Larry) Ogden, Pastor, church administrator, Executive Director, Reynolds Institute for Pastoral Education and Development.*

Usually one reads a book and wonders what the author is like. I have enjoyed the blessing of having it the other way around. Knowing Dallas as his pastor I have been impressed with the depth of his commitment to Christ and the searching nature of his insightful mind. These things combined with the deep well of experience gained through a remarkable professional life I was confident could lead to a very valuable book. "How I found the Riches of the Christian Life", will enrich you even as it has enriched me.

—Christopher Wiley, Senior Pastor, Dennis Church of the Nazarene Author, Professor of Philosophy, Ethics and Religion

An illuminating and engaging account of the Christian faith from a uniquely personal perspective which has much to offer those who read it.

—Larry Wilson, Pastor, Claremont, New Hampshire

Contents

I. A Personal Odyssey 19
    An Overdone Diplomatic Career 20
    How I Met Christ Despite Decades
    of Neglect 24
    Born Again 29
    What Followed 32

Photographs 39

II. Why Do We Need Religion? 43
    Instinctively We Accept God 43
    The Overwhelming Importance of
    Thinking It Through 43
    Distinctions Among Major Religions ...44

III. Creation 47
    The Universe 47
    How the Universe Came to Be 49
    When It Came to Be: Mankind, Dinosaurs
    and Other Creatures 53
    Conclusion 57

IV. God 59
    God and the Early Jews 60
    A Chosen People 61
    The Law Expanded 62

```
        Conclusion ............................................65
        Interlude ................................................65
        John the Baptist....................................66

  V.  Jesus of Nazareth ........................................69
        Prophecies ............................................71
        Miracles.................................................74
        Logic .....................................................76
        Timing ..................................................78
        Resurrection .........................................79
        Gospel Accounts ..................................80
        Crucifixion ...........................................85
        The Empty Tomb ................................86
        Resurrection Discovered ......................87
        The Reaction of the People ..................90
        Post-Resurrection Appearances ...........91
        More on the Reaction of the People......94
        Persecution Spreads .............................96
        Saul of Tarsus........................................99
        Others..................................................103
        Conclusion ..........................................106

 VI.  Implications ..............................................107
        God's Love – Our Love.......................107
        Our Love for Others ............................109
        The Prodigal Son.................................110
        The Kingdom of God and His Will.....113

VII. What Jesus Taught ........................................115
        The Kingdom of God ..........................115
        How to Find the Kingdom of God ......118
        Sermon on the Mount..........................123
```

	The Hard Saying	126
	Conclusion	129
VIII.	The Follow Through	131
	Sin: Consequences and Release	132
	The Role of the Cross	135
	Our Response	139
	Born Again	142
	The Holy Spirit	143
	The Holy Trinity	147
	Salvation	149
	God's Will	152
	Living the Riches of the Christian Life	153
	Heaven/Hell	157
	After the New Birth	159
	Finding the Right Way	164

Reading List 173
Notes on the Reading List 177

Acknowledgments

I have tried to express in early parts of this book my deep appreciation for Pastor Larry Ogden – what he has done for my life and for the urge to write this book. More recently he has joined others in suggesting how an earlier draft of the book could be meaningfully improved. I have also early in the book written of the extent which I have relied on the writings of others, many others.

It's a pleasure to add deep gratitude to Pastor Chris Wiley who eventually replaced Larry as pastor of our church. I had known some outstanding intellectuals in the course of my career, none, however, with a more brilliant intelligence than Pastor Chris Wiley, an author and teacher of philosophy while also a full-time, dedicated pastor. Busy as he is, he has given freely of his time to help make my manuscript a better book. He has brought others into discussions at which he provided direction and meaning. I have included in this book much that I have learned from his sermons and from conversations with him. He has been a cutting edge all the way.

It was Chris Wiley who encouraged our son, young Dallas, to participate much more outspokenly in attempts to enrich the text with bold, clear criticisms and suggestions, not always an easy task for any son, any father-son relationship; ours in fact grew closer. All this was made with his long history of writing as a political analyst and, now, as a teacher at Georgetown's Institute for the Study of Diplomacy. No other one helper has contributed so much to this book as young Dallas.

I would like, also, to thank our daughter-in-law, Liz, for the understanding and patience with which she has accepted her husband's long hours reviewing the manuscript.

The book has been decidedly a family affair. My wife, Gretchen, has given me crucial support. She steadfastly insists that I am intelligent. Though I know all evidence to be to the contrary, her confidence is a big help.

Our daughter, Alice, the most effective member of the family, has taken over wherever she's needed, coming forward with substantive ideas, always encouraging me, finding books and equipment that have helped, acting as a secretary, engaging in e-mail with other helpers. I could not have made it through the last push to get the manuscript ready without Alice.

I also want to thank Pastor Larry Wilson, now

Acknowledgments

pastor at Claremont, NH. In addition to committing drafts of the manuscript to computer disc, Larry has all along been warmly supportive. He and I have worked as a team. He has provided substantive material and his contribution has been vital.

CHAPTER I

A Personal Odyssey

This is a book about one man's journey in search of inner peace. Essentially, it offers a distillation of all I have learned through questions, debate and wide-ranged reading and research since the day I embraced Jesus Christ as Lord and Savior and was seized with an insatiable desire to learn and, subsequently, to tell others all I could about God.

It began as such things will, with a prelude. Our daughter, a born-again Christian who had been troubled, found a church and pastor that did much to see her through. At her request that pastor called a colleague whose church was near us. Thus we came to meet Pastor Larry Ogden. It is impossible for me to imagine a finer pastor — always a willing helper, always a pleasure, a listener who is knowledgeable and consistently guided by a deep love of God and an outstanding preacher with a remarkable talent to teach — a Godsend.

He came to my wife and me most opportunely. We had retired some years earlier. It had not been a golden retirement for me, though it should have been. I literally had it all — working as a writer when I chose, reading, landscaping and gardening. My problems were deep-seated and resulted from the way I had pursued my career.

At age twenty-three I had left a job that offered no rewards but took much from me. I spent four months wandering about Europe. Standing one evening at a corner of the Place de la Concorde in Paris without a dream that within little more than fifteen years I would be enthusiastically occupying a large, well furnished office at the American Embassy overlooking and within one hundred feet of where I meditated, I thought through the broad outlines of the kind of future I wanted.

Sooner than I hoped, all those goals had been met, including marriage to the girl I loved, and always will love, and two wonderful children. World War II provided a fruitful but perilous and uncomfortable interlude leading to a return to university and a hard go at reaching one of my fondest dreams — a career in the diplomatic service of the U.S. Department of State.

An Overdone Diplomatic Career

Like a dream come true such a career became mine and did, indeed, present progressively greater opportunities to serve my country. I loved it. I found I had a talent for international negotiations. I learned that the most effective negotiator is most likely to be the one who knows the subject matter better than anyone else in the room.

To intensity of work on such challenges was thus added incredibly long hours — six and one half days a week at well over the usual eight-hour workday. There were frequent occasions of working intensely until two-thirty in the morning, and returning to the office a few hours later — all over matters that I believed to be of real and lasting importance.

In terms of personal goals, my career had been a triumph. In terms of my physical state, especially my nerves, I was exhausted and depleted. Early retirement was a welcomed option. I had found the right career but neglected and lost sight of the kind of person I wanted to be. I was tense; I was impatient; I had far too little love left. I could not, try as I might, let go of the intensity with which I had pursued my career. I read the morning newspaper and dug in the soil with the same intensity as for decades I had met responsibilities considered directly related to the interest of my country.

There had been much satisfaction in my career, though at times social demands annoyed me. There is a legend among some in our diplomatic service that *Home Sweet Home* was written by an American diplomat who lived in our embassy in Paris and wrote his song one lonely Christmas Eve, "Mid pleasures and palaces. . . . there's no place like home." Research proved this legend to be premature. The author had indeed served as an American diplomat, but composed this song earlier.

The legend, nevertheless, seemed real to me. There were cocktail parties, dinner parties and receptions where we met some important and well-known people – presidents, prime ministers, a king, cabinet ministers, chairman of the Federal Reserve Board, many senators, congressmen, individuals like Adlai Stevenson and Eleanor Roosevelt, along with Hollywood stars.

There were pleasures and we were at times in palaces with incredible riches and glitter. It was a worldly life far beyond what I had sought or wanted. With considerable sadness, I submitted my written resignation at an early stage of my career. The work, however, was too rewarding and I allowed myself to be talked into withdrawing my resignation.

I was surprised to find that I was quite good at my work, especially as spokesman for my country at international conferences. Thus, I served as Chief of the American delegation to international conferences at Geneva and Tokyo. I later served for six years in Paris as permanent American delegate to an important international committee, the Economic Development and Review Committee (EDRC), where I eventually served as Chairman.

It was in this committee where the outlook for the economies and the policies intended to cope with problems foreseeable of each major industrial country were examined in a free exchange among delegates from other such countries, where conclusions were reached and published – all designed to avoid what in the inter-war period was labeled "beggar thy neighbor" policies. For me, it was a ball. I was the dominant figure on the committee and enjoyed every minute. As American delegate, I could always speak, but it was hard work at long hours, combined with a talent for timing and content in quick and free exchange, that drew close attention to what I had to say.

Circumstances finally led us to request a transfer back to the Department of State in Washington. Again, everything seemed to go my way. I had for some years by then been listed in *Who's Who in America* and *Who's Who Internationally*. More importantly, by that time I had made a name with important and influential people. Given a choice of positions, I joined the Secretary of State's Policy Planning Staff, where it was my job to look some three, five or more years ahead and recommend what policies might be considered. In this position, I was able to initiate and structure conferences to discuss policies I deemed of special importance to the Secretary of State and to sit in on his staff meetings from time to time. I was able to select from all over the country outstanding leaders, writers and speakers on the subject I had chosen. In this position I finally launched a long-held idea that led to the establishment of the Group of Seven, where at semi-annual meetings policies are freely discussed at the summit by leaders of the countries that most affect global relations and conditions. As a final assignment, I was lent to a White House committee to review and investigate certain long-held policies.

Taking into account that I had made it clear from the start that I didn't want to become an ambassador and that I had shunned political office of any kind, firmly rejecting pleas to take over the publication of a small, family newspaper on grounds it would lead me into politics . . . one would think I should have been content with the career I had. It had been, after all, everything I had wanted – everything. It left me empty. I had what the world had to offer. Worldly achievements and rewards left me cold.

I retired shortly before reaching the mandatory age and sought serenity through a much quieter life. Over the last three years of my career, my wife and I had spent vacations searching for an ideal house in an ideal location for our retirement. At the last minute we found and bought it in prestigious Chatham on Cape Cod. I had a bountiful income, more money than I had ever sought, and a loving family . . . but it was not enough.

One day one of the sweetest of our four grandchildren was quietly sobbing over something. I never found out what. I shouted at her, in effect, to get lost, to get out of my life.

I had hit bottom and realized it. Shakespeare's winter of discontent didn't begin to express where I found myself. (Some three years later that granddaughter and I were seated on the back steps into our garage when I told her about God's unconditional love. We had become loving friends.)

How I Met Christ Despite Decades of Neglect

It was shortly after hitting bottom that Pastor Larry Ogden began to visit with my wife and me, just talking, answering questions. Neither my wife nor I was a stranger to church. Each had been reared participating in church activities faithfully — I in the city, my wife in a small town nearby. Her church had been given to the town by her grandparents. Her father, its backbone, taught the adult Sunday School class, often the only service of the week. For two years I had even filled that role for him.

As far back as I can remember, I have always accepted that Jesus of Nazareth was and is Lord and Savior. I remember as a child getting on my knees before going to sleep to recite the simple prayer of childhood, "Now I lay me down to sleep . . . ." I remember going to church each Sunday with my brother to Sunday School and in the evenings attending the Epworth League for young boys at our church. I had never over that long period heard words like "born-again" or "unconditional love." Our churches didn't preach such things, or at least not enough to penetrate my possibly inattentive mind.

There was an unforgettable lesson in humility for me in teaching the Sunday School class of my father-in-law. One morning shortly before beginning class I was chatting with a few who had arrived early. The subject of Christmas arose. I stoutly and righteously declared that what we observe by Christmas is no less than the greatest event in history. The quiet voice of a meek and humble man said this was not so, that Easter observed such an occasion. Assuring my elderly friend that I, of course, believed firmly in the resurrection of our Lord, I asserted that even without it we would have had the teaching of Jesus. At this my friend let me have it, all in the same meek and friendly manner, possibly with the conviction learned from my father-in-law: had Jesus not fulfilled death on the cross and the resurrection he had foretold, he would have been a farce. Dumbfounded, and not for the last time, it came to me that my friend was right. I had never heard such truth and possibly, just possibly, I had much to learn.

There was still much to learn some forty years later when Pastor Larry Ogden began visiting us in our home. He answered when he could my incessant questions, and replied quietly, where appropriate, that he didn't have answers. I was impressed also by his willingness to accept without comment my ludicrous statement that I had no sins. He knew that only the Holy Spirit convicts us of sins.

I won't try to repeat here just what Larry said to us. It was long ago. He always spoke calmly; he made his points out of an experience and study I lacked. There was nothing bizarre or eccentric; it was the Bible told straight. He taught us that finding the true Christian life required a far deeper commitment than mere acceptance of Jesus, that receiving the Holy Spirit through the new birth was a prerequisite. After that, reading, understanding, living in accordance with the Bible would come naturally. I had no doubts that he was right, that a life-saving exercise was involved if I, too, could only be born again and follow the guidance of the Holy Spirit through faith in Jesus Christ.

Thus began my prayer life. I wanted above

A Personal Odyssey

anything the new birth and I prayed hard. I prayed that I didn't seek to have any jewels in my crown (remembering an old hymn) but would gladly shine shoes if only I could be with Jesus. I record this with no attempt at humor or any feeling of superiority. I feel the same way today, but I wouldn't refuse any reward should it be offered.

With the Holy Spirit in me, I became an avid reader of the Bible. I had tried to read the Bible, starting with the Sermon on the Mount, early in my retirement only to find it all too tedious. Now, with the new birth I couldn't get enough of it.

We began attending Larry's church and a Sunday School class he was teaching. Within a very few weeks we learned truths that we had missed over decades. Larry was the one who urged me to write a book on what I had learned. When I protested that my knowledge was far too scant to try to help others, he began guiding me toward the best books to read. This I was already engaged in. I pursued it enthusiastically. I had always loved reading. But here was a new life of learning.

It is, thus, on the knowledge of more learned and gifted writers that most of this book is based. My indebtedness to others would be hard to overstate. It is their views, facts and comments that brought a sense of fulfillment to me and that I have here assembled in a way designed to present the most carefully prepared and thorough witness to God I have been able to muster. It is my great hope that readers will accept the special effort I have made to weigh the available evidence as objectively as I can

— to look at the facts available as in a trial-by-jury — before reaching conclusions.

Throughout this book, the source for Bible references is given in the text; details of other sources are in the Reading List at the end of the book.. Some writers had a particularly strong impact, and my comments about them are also incorporated in the Reading List at the end of the text. Each author drawn upon in what follows has much to reward readers. We do well to keep in mind, however, that each is human; none is without fault, as each would agree.

Many of these writers, for example, succumb to the instinct that what plays for one must play for all. Yet most of us could, for example, be divided into those who are early-morning persons and those who are not. Preachers and writers of early morning habits are inclined to urge that the real time for the most serious prayer of the day is early morning, the earlier the better. Yet, to God it's always morning or evening or night, for he is everywhere. My experience has been that what God wants is prayer at any time — indeed at all times as often as we like — but prayer with the right attitude toward him; that's when our prayers are at their best.

Nearer to the point at hand, some writers and some pastors embrace the view that the Bible was written under the active inspiration of the Holy Spirit of God, that Scripture is inerrant. Jesus held this view throughout his ministry. Paul wrote in his second letter to Timothy (3:16), "All Scripture is God-breathed." There are places where this is hard to accept, but I'm convinced that it's not only the right position; it is the more comfortable one; otherwise, one is left to make crucial decisions of what is authentic in the Bible and what is not. Amazing differences can arise from such decisions, along with uncertainty where there is no place for it. The Bible is the anchor of faith. I start with the assumption that there should be no question as to its total reliability.

Born Again

This humanness among writers comes through, too, in another way. Each commentator tends, however unwittingly, to assume that his spiritual experiences — the new birth, for example — are those that without exception all must experience. To me, this is just not the way God works. To him we are each individuals. In his infinite knowledge and wisdom he knows our background, our strengths and weaknesses, our individual needs. What he gives is best for each of us.

The Apostle Paul had such a traumatic experience on being born again that he was blind for three days. He wrote of that experience often, but never in an effort to imply that his experience must be for all as it was for him.

In my own experience, as one example, after praying to Jesus over a period of three days he came. Knowing my skepticism and other weaknesses, he came dramatically.

After lunch on that afternoon I was reading a novel. I put it down, lay across a bed and fell asleep while praying to Jesus for the new birth. I awoke with a strong and wonderful feeling of warmth throughout my torso, like warm running waters. I sat quietly for hours, relishing the sensation in strange contentment. The Spirit had come! I was born again. At last there was a new meaning and a new anchor in my life, one that would lead me to inner peace.

The Apostle Paul wrote that when we are born again we are made new creations. My experience was that all my wants in every detail had instantly made a 180-degree turn. There was the glow of that inner feeling that supreme and dependable help was with me and would make me what God knows is best for me.

The Spirit has never left me, never let me down. (He has by now filled me.) Above all he is still changing me. With kindness, hope and conviction he brought home to me a list of what was wrong with me, the sins and resulting feeling of guilt. Instant forgiveness by grace through faith is always there, so long as we are truly penitent, and ask in Jesus' name. In my experience I have found myself often struggling with old habits — the scars of old, though forgiven sins — at a diminishing rate.

The need to confess and receive forgiveness, though diminishing, is still with me. Love, faith and hope are with me increasingly. I began from the first and continue to read Scripture, pray and study commentaries on the Bible, all out of an inner urge of excitement that continues. If this book reaches the hands of others, it is by the Spirit, not by me.

In contrast to my own experience, I know from

personal observation that others have received the new birth with no drama. Quietly, they have felt a new assurance, a new desire to love God and a new attraction to the Bible and devotional material.

Billy Graham, surely the greatest evangelist of our time — considering the number of people he reaches, arguably the greatest of any time — has in television interviews described his own experience of the new birth. While still a teenager, attending a revival meeting out of curiosity, the call was made for those who wanted Christ in their lives to come forward for special prayer. Inexplicably, he felt an urge to go forward. He did, and left the meeting knowing that he had made the conversion, although he felt no special sensations confirming it.

Through faith that what was promised would be done, he went on, accepting that he was born again. He had conviction, courage and faith. He was right; that is what is required. Those qualities must have stood him in good stead when he scheduled his first appearance and went out, possibly to an empty stadium, hall or open field, and preached.

Why the difference in experiences? God knew that I had reached a point where drama was needed to overcome the odd combination of arrogance and cynicism with recognized helplessness. God knows best what we need. His understanding, his compassion, his help to the helpless are amazing in their abundance. God is love.

A final comment on personal experiences in prayer. The new birth in my case brought with it a love for Jesus that was overwhelming, warm, comforting — head over heels. All my prayers were to him in his name's sake. After some months I observed a gentle, but insistent push to pray to the Father, in Jesus' name, as Jesus did. It was like a curtain gently and firmly closed. I sensed that it was to God the Father, in Jesus' name, I should pray. This went well for some years. Then came another gentle and insistent push to include also worship of the Holy Spirit. He in turn has led me to love all the more the one God in three persons — Father, Son, and Holy Spirit.

My initial overwhelming love of Jesus is stronger; my love has become great enough to extend without diminishment to the Father, Son, and Holy Spirit. My role in this was to pray as my heart directed, otherwise remaining passive.

What Followed

I have for reasons I don't know always wanted my major time in prayer to be at the end of the day and evening. Early in my new prayer life the Holy Spirit began and has continued to make himself felt within me as I am in prayer whatever the time of day. I am, of course, overwhelmed with gratitude for this. I felt I should never end prayer as long as this feeling was in me — you don't walk out while God is speaking to you. This didn't work. The feeling never left until I had said my Amen. In time the Spirit has let me know that, for me at my age, several short periods in prayer are better than one or two long periods.

A Personal Odyssey

Yet, I reached a time some five years ago when to my horror I began yawning while in prayer. I tried several remedies. They failed. Finally, after a yawn in the middle of prayer time I confessed to God my extreme distress and personal inability to handle the wrong. I asked in Jesus name for God's help. There have been no more yawns since.

More recently I became convinced that my prayers were stilted. I was uneasy while walking through some woods one morning. I prayed (thought mail), "Holy Spirit, please tell me how I can improve the quality of my prayer life." The response was a clear and instant, "Just talk."

I relate these experiences to encourage others to realize the incredible goodness of God's grace. He receives; he understands; and he acts in ways that he knows are best.

Those who have read the epistles of the Apostle Paul will possibly have noted how boldly at times he boasted of himself. He acknowledged this and explained that such boasting was for Christ, to achieve the confidence of readers that his teachings of Christ were authentic. And so it is that a few friends, for whom I have special respect, have persuaded me to boast about myself in this my own effort to win souls to Christ. Thus, some boasting about my career and spiritual life are given above and more is now to come as I write of my most sacred experiences.

Twice Jesus has appeared to me quite clearly. The first such occasion was on the day my wife had her first heart attack. The local doctor had identified the problem and summoned the ambulance. Deeply disturbed and afraid, I drove to the hospital emergency room to be with her. After she had been settled comfortably in the intensive care unit and I had been assured that she was in good hands, I was driving home. I was furious, tears running down my cheek. How dare this serious threat to the wife I so loved, the wife who had stayed by me all my adult life? Suddenly a feeling of quiet came over me. It seemed that someone was with me, was going to see me through. I stole a glance to my right. Jesus was there, physically there, in the seat beside me. He spoke no words, his gaze was fixed calmly on the road ahead. He was just letting me know that he was there with me all the way. I was at peace.

As I took the exit off the throughway to Chatham, Jesus disappeared. Yet some days later, I was again uneasy. I asked Pastor Larry Ogden how I should pray. I remember well his instant response, "Dal, if you pray the prayer of Gethsemane I guarantee that God's will will prevail." Wow! Enormous relief overcame me. I had come to appreciate that God knows the future as well as the present and past and that God loves us. I prayed as Larry had suggested the prayer of Gethsemane which is, of course, the prayer Jesus offered at the spot of that name just before the guards came to take him to the incredibly, inhumane and cruel punishment up to and including the cross. As this moment was at hand, Jesus prayed, "Father, if you are willing, take this cup from me; yet not my will, but yours be done" (Luke 22:42).

A Personal Odyssey

Some two or three years later, Jesus appeared to me again, and that time we actually conversed. It must have been a little after five in the afternoon. I was operating our rider mower. All lawns had been cut but one, a favorite in a back patch of our property. Glancing up I saw Jesus come out of a narrow path leading downhill to a water well. His walk was casual; as before he was wearing a white (not dazzling white as in special appearances in the Bible) tunic, light brown beard and long hair. His walk was so casual it occurred to me that he had called it a day and was on his way home. It was as though on seeing me he changed course and came toward me. Though he had been two to three hundred feet away, still walking casually, he was beside me instantly.

"Hello, Dallas," he said.

My jaw must have been sagging. The mower had ceased operating the moment I saw him. I slid from the seat, dropped to one knee and in awe replied, "Lord!"

"I have come to take you with me," he said.

Stunned and totally flabbergasted, I was speechless. "Does this not please you?" he asked.

"Ecstatically so," I finally got out; hesitantly and stammering I said, "But, Lord, what about Gretchen (my wife)? She needs me."

"Not to worry," he replied, comforting me. "After I have taken you, I'll come back for her."

"Then, Lord," I exclaimed, "let us go!"

Suddenly it was all over. Jesus had disappeared. The rider mower was operating as before, but I was more deeply touched than at any time in my life. It's an episode or illusion that keeps recurring to me. What was the meaning?

Looking back over my life, a miraculously close encounter with death during the Normandy invasion and other close encounters, I feel God has a plan for me. Could it be to win souls for Christ? By means of this book? I'm trying. And he's still with me all the way – Father, Son and Holy Spirit.

In the book that follows, I have devoted some attention to the nature of the Holy Trinity. For some it is easy to accept without question the simple fact that there is one God and he is in three persons, distinct but inseparably one. For others it can be a significant problem, for example, to whom to address prayers, with whom to converse, and on whom to think between prayers. God's grace, which can neither be deserved nor bought, but which is given so freely through faith, resolves all problems in God's own gentle way and timing. He wants us to learn more about his will for us; our response is to love, worship and persevere.

The words of the hymn, "He Giveth His Grace," tell it well:

> His love has no limit, His grace has no measure;
> His pow'r has no boundary known unto men.
> For out of His infinite riches in Jesus,
> He giveth, and giveth, and giveth again.
> — *Annie Johnson Flint*

And he has done and is doing so much for me that I am prepared to give everything to help others find his peace and joy.

Photographs

The author in phases of his career.

At Geneva

How I Found the Riches of the Christian Life

At Madrid

Photographs

At Paris with Dr. Paul McCracken, member of President Nixon's cabinet, at a conference on economic policy at the cabinet level.

(Insertion reads "To Dallas Jones, with deep appreciation to an esteemed colleague for his unstinting labors on behalf of a better international economy and with best wishes.")

At Paris, as Chairman about to open a conference on economic policy.

CHAPTER II

Why Do We Need Religion?

Instinctively We Accept God

All of us at one time or another — before being wheeled into the operating room, while sitting beside a sick child or spouse — have experienced that urge to lift our eyes with stumbling words of prayer to some superior being with power, love and compassion beyond the best that is human. Inwardly we know there must be a better life hereafter (though we're not really certain it's for us) and that this superior being holds the key.

The Overwhelming Importance of Thinking Through

The central proposition of this book is that if

there exists such a superior being even though we acknowledge him only when in danger, then learning all we can about that being is the most important single need in our lives. We might find, as one example, that the superior being doesn't even receive our prayers when they are sent, so to speak, in an unadressed, unstamped envelope. Such a being has a right to expect us to make an effort. And, he has shown us the way.

Which way? Which superior being? I know, of course, that more than one is pursued in our multinational, multicultural world. A cursory look at the principal religions might be useful.

Distinctions Among Major Religions

Judaism is an integral part of Christianity, though the reverse is not the case. The Bible's Old Testament (central to Judaism) is to the Christian a prophecy and introduction to the New Testament which is fully embraced by Christians. Judaism centers on the Ten Commandments and the more detailed instructions God gave to the Jews as the Law. Unfortunately, and some time later, Jewish priests added much onerous detail; God's law became and remains man-made law (still regarded as the Law). Followers of Judaism still await the coming of the Messiah, an event foreseen by Jewish prophets of old.

Christians believe the Messiah came about two thousand years ago, just as prophesied; that he came in the person of Jesus Christ; that, as prophesied, he

Why Do We Need Religion?

was crucified and died on the cross to pay for our sins; that he was resurrected from the dead three days later and still later ascended to and remains with God, his Father. They believe that faith in Jesus Christ as Lord leads to inner peace now and to eternal salvation. Love and grace supercede the Law. In fewest words the Christian message is: Jesus saves.

Islam adopts certain aspects from Judaism and Christianity. Muslims believe that Allah sent messengers, including Abraham, Moses, Jesus and Mohammed (ca 570-632). Mohammed claimed neither Jesus nor he was divine; the message of Jesus was good, but he failed to force its success by political skill and military means; Mohammed did. Muslims emphasize legalism, mysticism and fate.

These three religions are considered God-revealed; others man-revealed. Similarities among different religions give some credence to the concept that we are all born with instincts to look for a god. I conclude, however, that it would be fatal to fall into the acceptance that they're all the same, that distinctions don't matter, that we just need to accept that there's a god and "do right" or something equally vague. That's a path that leads to unaddressed (or wrongly addressed) envelopes, to unanswered prayers and a life without conviction and meaning. God is too important for effortless vagueness.

I believe there is no call for vagueness or mystery here. I have written this book in the firm belief that Christianity, thus the Christian God, is the only means to life to the full now and eternal salvation thereafter. In what follows, I will make every effort to present grounds for this conclusion as objectively as possible.

CHAPTER III

Creation

∽

At the heart of my initial questions on the existence of God is how the universe was created and whether man was created or whether he evolved from whatever living thing first somehow appeared.

The Universe

I discovered that there remains much about the universe that we do not know, just as we do not understand the length of infinity or the duration of eternity. I reviewed a good contemporary encyclopedia to learn the basics.

Our own galaxy contains more than 100 billion stars, of which our sun is one, grouped in a giant circular shape; that the distance across this one galaxy is about 100,000 light years and that one light year is almost six trillion miles. Studies indicate that there are at least 100 billion galaxies in the universe, although anyone would be hard pressed to make a firm statement on the vastness of the universe. For example, quasars may be as far away as 10 billion light years, that is 10 billion times 5.88 trillion miles. At some point most of us will just give up on vastness.

The speed at which observed galaxies travel is estimated to vary from about 700 miles a second to 90,000 miles a second. The shape of observed galaxies varies from spiral to elliptical to irregular.

The rough picture, then, is of countless stars clustered together but moving at great speed and of countless clusters racing about in a space that is too vast to comprehend. All this started and has continued running since the beginning

It was not just an empty universe that emerged. Here on earth, at least, there are the living, breathing things we now observe. There are also remains of older, no longer present living things archaeologists have unearthed.

We can observe that earth's living inhabitants from the tiniest to the largest are constituted and enabled to reproduce with a complexity that boggles the mind. Think, for example, of a flea's digestive tract and think of the complexities and capabilities of the human mind with its memory. And then there are plants from grass on the lawn to giant trees. They regularly feed and for the most part reproduce themselves and it goes on and on.

I first tried to come to grips with who created the universe and, then, the age of the universe.

Creation

How the Universe Came to Be

There are, generally speaking, two schools of thought on how creation came about. One view is quite clear, the Biblical view. It holds that God created the universe and all on it (Genesis 1-2) and that he did this at a time and in a way of his choosing.

Most other views center around a belief that creation was brought about by some event like a big bang occurring in space somewhere at some time.

Among those holding this view, some believe that the "big bang" was brought on by some superior, supernatural being but not God, not as we know him. Einstein came to hold this view (*The Fingerprint of God,* 171). Darwin believed that living things were started by the Christian God and then evolved (*Darwin,* 261; Bible Difficulties, 557). Then there are those who believe that it all "just happened."

I discern movement among scientists toward acceptance of God as creator. Several opinion polls indicate this. An article published in *Scientific American* (September 99) indicates that about 40 percent of scientists believe in God.

As I delved into the different theories, I was struck by an analogy written by William Paley, who some two hundred years ago authored a two-volume classic on moral philosophy and other works. He wrote of a man walking in strange and isolated parts who saw lying at his feet a watch. He had never before seen a watch. He examined it closely with amazement at its complexity, precision and its predetermined order. He knew at once that somewhere there was a person who made watches.

I saw that Paley's tale showed the reaction of common sense to something otherwise unintelligible. The man could have concluded that somewhere in time the many varied and rare parts observed had – against all odds – fallen into place and begun operating to apparent perfection and limitless time. Surely, in our search for truth about the universe, common sense must rule; searching for complexities is unnecessary and unproductive.

I picked up the first book I had ever seen by C. S. Lewis, *Mere Christianity*, at a sale of used paperbacks. I read it and have reread in many times. This first copy is now in shreds, so I bought another copy. I am always struck by the simplicity with which he presented great, deep, and vital truths. Lewis began contemplating the relative merits of each view on creation while still an atheist under pressure from some of his fellow professors at Oxford to accept God's existence. In the process he became, with reluctance, a dedicated believer in God, then in Jesus Christ. The results of his reasoning (the Biblical view of Creation) is in the first chapter of his book, *Miracles – A Preliminary Study*. I find his reasoning practical, straight to the point and completely persuasive. I have drawn heavily from it, along with views of others, in what follows.

Logic tells us that no complete system, a watch, a universe, a factory or a house can create itself; there must be a concept and a start from without. Given its vastness and complexities, the universe had to be started by a supernatural being. Lewis

Creation

decided that only the creator God could do it. Who or what else?

Lewis went on to conclude that God, the creator, had to be benevolent, for we all instinctively know that God is good, and good is good, and bad is bad.

Amusingly, Lewis wrote of overhearing two people, one complaining that the other had done something wrong. The argument that followed, he wrote, was not over whether the act in question was good or bad, right or wrong. Agreement over that was implied. The retort of the accused was that he/she didn't do it or couldn't help it. Haven't we all engaged in or witnessed such exchanges?

The view I draw from the Bible is that if the vastness and complexity of the universe leave one feeling insignificant, that is only because of overemphasis on measurement; the individual is precious; each one is born — as Adam and Eve were created — with a soul or spirit in the image of God. That is, to put it simply, each individual is born with instincts that good is good and bad is bad.

Immanuel Kant, eminent German philosopher, in his *Critique of Practical Reason*, observed,

> Two things fill the mind with ever-increasing wonder and awe . . . the starry heavens above me and the moral law within me.

Thus we have a collective and individual sense of moral justice — what is decent, what is right and fair. These are patterns of thought — along with the reasoning process of thinking, itself — that could hardly be explained without a supernatural source of direction, that is, a source outside the system of nature. Nature on its own just cannot be the source of the kinds of moral judgments we all consciously or subconsciously engage in. It has no moral judgment of its own. Billy Graham has put it that a mother's love has never been reproduced in a laboratory.

Thus we have a voice within — a conscience. Thus we have guilt complexes, longings and dissatisfaction with ourselves.

Augustine, a Christian writer at the turn of the fourth century, had one of the great minds of all time. He put it this way: " Thou hast created us for thyself, and our heart cannot be quieted till it may find repose in thee." (*Confessions*, Book 1, Chapter I, first paragraph). I am particularly pleased to insert this thought here out of concern that I may earlier have left the view that God may be needed only by those who have "hit bottom." Augustine knew and wrote that we all need God.

Augustine reasoned that without God we have strife. We quickly develop self-centeredness and self-will, yet we are born with a spirit seeking justice, honor, peace, love, helping others, and the like. This strife is found at the international level, where combinations of mistrust and self-will overcome a sense of honor and trust, leading to war. It is found at the national level in injustices, riots, crimes, and drug trafficking, etc. It is found — perhaps above all — within each person. There is within each person a civil war raging between self-will and the implanted concepts of love, honor, decency, fair play that we somehow know are right. The result is strife and more strife.

Dr. Olive Winchester wrote in *The Story of the Old Testament* that since creation man has been and is repeatedly tested and found wanting. This is the individual struggle with strife.

Although since Adam and Eve we are born in the image of God, we are also given from birth free will. Apparently God has no interest in a world of robots who love him automatically. How our will is directed — to God or self-centeredness— determines how we cope with strife.

When The Universe Came To Be: Mankind, Dinosaurs and Other Creatures

But what about the age of the universe, the dinosaurs and other ancient fossils one reads of? There is controversy over the age of the universe and, thus, of the earth. Some, for example the Institute of Creation Research, believe the earth to be relatively young, compared to estimates of others who consider archeological finding as evidence that the universe is about 16 billion years old.

The Bible nowhere gives an age for creation's beginning.

I came upon an intriguing concept that, if accepted, might help clarify (or defuse) what may be pointless debate over when creation occurred and thus to explain what appear to be extremely ancient remains sometimes unearthed. In this there are differences among those of the Biblical view of creation. Some hold the view that the Bible is inerrant, that it is inspired throughout by God and that any manipulation is unacceptable (and there is much in favor of this view).

Yet others, including some who accept total inerrancy, read the first two chapters of the Bible in a way that, in their view, involves no manipulation and has led them to introduce a concept called theistic evolution, that is, a form of evolution created by God.

The central point in theistic evolution is in how we read the first two chapters of Genesis. And it relates to time involved in creation of the earth and of Adam and Eve – how many days, or might it have been billions of years? How we read the word "day" seems to be what it all rests on.

Those who support a form of theistic evolution point out that centuries before the question of evolution became so heated, scholars and many early church leaders had assumed that the creation period related in the Bible was a very long period of time. Among them are Josephus, the first century Jewish historian, Irenaeus, Origen, Augustine and Aquinas (*The Fingerprint of God*, 141).

More recently, some scholars have added details to this theory of creation – specifically how much time may have been involved and what might have happened in the period of creation, *Encyclopedia of Bible Difficulties*, 56-65).

As far back as the turn of the past century Dr. C.I. Scofield in his commentary on Isaiah 45:18

(itself written in the eighth century B. C.) suggested that this was one of the Biblical passages that might be taken as evidence that at some stage or stages before Adam and Eve God may have laid waste to the earth and then recreated it.

Dr. Gleason Archer in his *Encyclopedia of Bible Difficulties* expands substantially on the proposition of theistic evolution. He writes that the original Hebrew used in the first chapters of the Bible and in the Isaiah passage cited above should not necessarily be read to mean that God created the earth and all thereon in six twenty-four-hour days as is commonly assumed, but within stages of creation. (pp. 63).

It may be noted that even today in contemporary usage words can have different meanings. We might say, as a ready example, "This was a lovely day, " and mean about twelve hours; we might say, "In the early day of hand-to-hand warfare, casualties were fewer," and mean an extended period of time.

I can't help but think that those who persist in fixing their eyes on small details (the trees) risk missing the big picture (the forest). So it is that perhaps too many focus on the proposition that the Bible says that God created Adam twenty-four hours after creating earth (which it does not say) and too easily give up on reconciling their reasoning with the Bible.

Those who support the concept of theistic evolution suggest that errors could have been the work of prehistoric things, including rebellion of any prehistoric human types. The Bible specifically presents one instance (the flood) when God saw a need to eliminate all but one family of mankind (Genesis 6 and 7) – with the clear promise of a more thorough change (the return of Christ) in the future.

[Those who more readily put confidence in the New Testament can find the flood and Noah referred to by Jesus (Luke 17:26) and others (Hebrews 11:7, I Peter 3:20 and II Peter 2:5).]

Under this proposition, one could accept any age for the earth and any kind of creature from dinosaurs to prehistoric man not made in the image of God, all according to this concept, existing before Adam and Eve, leaving their fossils for future scientists to discover.

Dr. Hugh Ross, a man with degrees in science, physics and astronomy, who for several years continued research of quasars and galaxies as a post-doctoral fellow at the California Institute of Technology, has published evidence that the Biblical account of creation is correct. His book, *The Fingerprint of God*, comprises some 200 pages on the subject. The final sentence of his book summarizes his conclusions:

Though much more remains to be researched and discussed about cosmology and its theological implications, the only rational response to the mountain of evidence accumulated thus far is to surrender one's life to the God of the Bible.

Along the way, Dr. Ross points out that the Bible is the only religious text that presents a cosmology in full agreement with the latest astrophysical discoveries.

Conclusion

My conclusion is that creation of the universe was a supernatural event, and that the author of that event is God, a supernatural spiritual being.

We do well when new discoveries are made that appear inconsistent with the Bible to hold to the assumption that the Bible is right; that in time the new discovery will be reconciled to it, that essentially what is being searched for is how God went about doing things his way. This has been the way of new discoveries in the past; it is not likely to change.

Of course it's not easy to visualize and thus to accept that God created the universe and all that's in it. But in terms of sheer plausibility isn't it much harder to accept that it all "just happened"?

CHAPTER IV

God

～

Have I so far provided any grounds we can begin to use to know what God is like? Yes, some certainly. If God created the universe and all that's on it, he is infinite — ponder that word, please — in power, wisdom and knowledge. Moreover, he created us to sense what is good and what is bad - to have a conscience - and to feel wrong when we should. From this I see proof that God is benevolent.

From reading the Bible, I am convinced that God has always wanted us to know him, has always wanted each one of us to have the opportunity to know him, to make the choice between being self - centered or God-centered.

He started with the people of Israel. Before literacy, they passed experiences with and knowledge of him orally from generation to generation. Take a look at what follows from the first verse of Psalm 78:

What we have heard and known,
What our fathers have told us,
We will not hide them from our children,
We will tell the next generation
the praiseworthy deeds of the Lord,
his power, and the wonders he has done.

God and the Early Jews

God found particularly pleasing the faith in him of Abram (later called Abraham). Abraham was from Ur of the Chaldeans, a large center of commerce south of the present-day Baghdad and peopled by idol-worshipers. He moved with his wife to Haran, a city northwest of Damascus and settled there for a time. Abraham continued to move about under God's instructions, living a semi-nomadic life and prospering in Canaan, the Negev, Egypt and back to Canaan.

God told Abraham he would make him the father of countless descendants. At that time, it is worth noting, there was no distinction between Jew and Gentile. Through Abraham the nation of Israel was formed and set apart as the first through which the knowledge, acceptance and worship of the one true God was to be passed to many nations (Genesis 17:4). In the sight of God, Abraham is the father of all who believe in God (Romans 4:17).

In early days God taught the Jews not to marry outsiders, for worship of idols by outsiders was prevalent, and the Jews were to resist it. On their own, the Jews adopted an intense, almost fierce, clannishness and were disliked by others for it. They were twice conquered and for long periods dispersed into exile.

The Romans, who became military occupiers of Israel, finally found the Jews too rebellious. The New Testament records that, on overlooking Jerusalem, Jesus wept and prophesied that the city would be horribly destroyed (Luke 19:43). It was some forty years later (A.D. 70) that in anger the Romans sacked the city, leaving it so devastated that a plough was drawn across the middle of it.

Many Jews remain scattered around the world. The intensity of holding their common ancestry, culture and nationality is a common theme binding them together. Like others, the Jews are and were individuals, not always thinking or acting alike.

A Chosen People

While the Jews were God's chosen people, they were not without human frailty. Like other nations, they were not monolithic. Many of them could not accept that they were only temporarily the guardians of the knowledge of God and of our relationship with him. Over time the feeling grew that they and only they were God's chosen people, once and forever. Yet God had repeatedly reminded them through his prophets — and in person through Abraham — that at the right time the Jews would share him with other nations — willingly if possible, but share him, for example:

... make known to the nations what he has done and proclaim that his name is exalted ... for he has done glorious things; let this be known to all the world (Isaiah 12:4-5).

The Law Expanded

Blind insistence, chiefly by priests and other leaders, that Israel was forever the only chosen people, was boosted by the rise to power within the Jewish religious establishment of sects that asserted that only their views were acceptable. Through them the law God dictated to Moses, which had governed Jewish life over the centuries, was enlarged and distorted into a mass of incredibly detailed "dos and don'ts." It was concerned overwhelmingly with how people must carry out daily lives and observe their Sabbath — man-made externalities of worshiping God.

Professor William Barclay, in his commentary on Matthew 5:17-20, described some aspects in this massively detailed law of what constitutes work forbidden on the Sabbath. A few extracts of Barclay's description give the flavor.

It is forbidden on the Sabbath day to carry:

> Food equal in weight to a dried fig,
> enough wine for mixing in a goblet,
> milk enough for one swallow,
> honey enough to put upon a wound,
> water enough to moisten an eye salve,

> paper enough to write a customs
> house notice upon,
> ink enough to write two letters of the
> alphabet,
> reed enough to make a pen.

Barclay added that, to the Orthodox Jew "religion, serving God, was a matter of keeping thousands of legalistic rules and regulations; they regarded these petty rules and regulations as literally matters of life and death and eternal destiny" (130).

The arrogance of the new orthodox, chiefly the Pharisees and Sadducees, on how God must be worshiped was such that it placed impossible burdens on ordinary people. Yet failure to obey brought the threat of being cast off, in effect, excommunicated.

Moreover, women in the Middle East were still being treated as little more than cattle. This was contrary to God's law given to Moses, but had come to be accepted in part through the influence of foreigners. If, for example, a man wanted to divorce his wife, he had only to testify in writing that she no longer pleased him. Alimony? It didn't exist.

Corruption and political intrigue grew. Since God, as a father-teacher, has always insisted that sins must be paid for, animal sacrifices to God were made at the Temple — the prevailing means of atonement for sins. Such animals — for example sheep, doves — had to pass inspection as pure and unblemished by Temple officials responsible to the high priest. The only sure way to have an acceptable offering was to buy it from approved sellers at the Temple. The animal might not be pure, but the price for it was fixed to profit the Temple establishment.

God, through his prophet Isaiah, had informed the nation of Israel that he could no longer endure animal sacrifices as atonement for sin. Those sacrificing were not sincere; the Jews were to stop depending on sacrifices and learn to avoid sin. (Isaiah 1:10-17).

God was regarded increasingly as both isolated and remote. It was believed that God resided primarily within the confines of an elaborate and beautiful man-made area; more and more attention was being focused on the law in all its massive detail, less and less on God Himself.

The ordinary Jew could come only to the gate of the Tabernacle court. The priests and Levites could enter the court, but only the priests entered regularly the outer room, and only the high priest, on special occasions, could briefly enter the inner room where it was believed by too many that God resided.

Where was the God of love and omnipresence that David worshiped? Priests kept him hidden.

The Bible teaches, perhaps most specifically in Jeremiah 31:34, but throughout the Old and New Testaments, that at a time of his choosing God will once more make at least a remnant of the Jews his special people and that Jews and Gentiles will come together in worship of him.

Conclusion

This much we can surely add to what God is like: he is incredibly patient and forbearing. Some years ago I happened upon a TV interview with Jackie Gleason. Did he believe in God? Yes. What did he know about him? "Well," he replied, "he must be patient; he's put up with us all these years." And so I conclude from this chapter.

There is one source who, if credible, can tell us all about God. This source is Jesus of Nazareth. All that follows will be about him and what he taught.

Interlude

The last book in the Old Testament was written by the prophet Malachi, who wrote in the fifth century B.C. Through Malachi, God expressed extreme displeasure over the priests of the Temple and over what the people in general had become. The priests were corrupt and inept, causing many to stumble in their relationship with God; the people were miserly and sinful, notably in their treatment of family. God instructed Malachi to voice these criticisms all over Israel (Malachi 1:1-6, 13-14; 2:13-14).

Malachi is most known, however, for his prophecy about God's messenger, "See I will send my messenger, who will prepare the way before me" (Malachi 3:1).

Several centuries earlier God had informed Isaiah and he had written that at a future time there would be a voice of one calling in the desert,

"Prepare the way for the Lord, make straight in the wilderness a highway for our God" (Isaiah 40:3).

John the Baptist

It was over 400 years after Malachi that Jesus of Nazareth was born. For all these years the Jews had been without God's chosen spokesmen, prophets. They were wondering among themselves when another prophet might be sent to them, for prophets, though often reviled during their lives, were seen as a reassurance that the Jews were still God's chosen people.

Into this background and environment John the Baptist made his entrance. It was dramatic.

The son of a Temple priest, a devout one, John scorned life among the establishment and lived an almost savage life in the desert wilderness across the Jordan River. Near Jerusalem he preached aggressively, "Repent, for the kingdom of heaven is near."

When asked who he was, John replied in the words of Isaiah, "I am the voice of one calling in the desert, 'Make straight the way for the Lord'" (John 1:23). Despite the man-made burdens placed on their pursuit of God, the people of Israel maintained a fearful awe and worship of God. Thus, large crowds gathered and were baptized by John. They asked if at last they had received a prophet from God or perhaps even in John the long-awaited Messiah (Christ).

John proclaimed himself as nothing more than a forerunner of the Christ, "the thongs of whose sandals I am not worthy to untie" (Luke 3:16).

Most people, at least in Europe and the Americas, accept that Jesus of Nazareth lived and taught generally as written in the Bible. Not as many accept his divinity. In the next chapter I will explore that specific question.

CHAPTER V

Jesus of Nazareth

∞

Almost 2,000 years ago Jesus walked from his carpenter's home in Nazareth to the spot some 80 miles south where John the Baptist interrupted his cries to the crowds of Jews to point at Jesus and proclaim to his listeners that there stood the long-awaited Son of God, the Christ, (Messiah in Hebrew) of prophecies extending from the first to the last book of the Bible.

What drama! Among the large crowd present were many devoted to God. They stood in awe of God and his power. They and their ancestors had awaited the Christ over generations, centuries. They were zealous in worship, but lacking in knowledge of what God had taught them through his prophets. They knew God as accessible only through the hierarchy of priests with animal sacrifices. They believed anyone who happened to see God's face (unthinkable) would immediately die.

They had come to picture the Christ as one who would be a king like David, driving all enemies to destruction by military might, even overthrowing the Roman Empire. They were highly emotional about all this. They had walked for miles to hear John, an awesome personality feared even by King Herod. They heard and saw John as he pointed and said in effect, "There, right there, is the Christ you have been waiting for." They would have instantly fallen to the ground, faces down in awe and fear.

Jesus, sensing high emotion and clamor for a Christ who would rule militarily, slipped quietly out of sight. He had no wish to be the center of a military rebellion against the Roman occupiers of Israel or against any others.

After forty days of meditation and prayer, Jesus launched a three-year ministry and suffered the cruelest death known to man. The world would never be the same. In that brief span, never leaving a country about 150 miles long and an average of about 70 miles in width, Jesus changed the whole course of history. To this day we divide history into two parts, before and after Christ.

If he was (is) who he said he is, Jesus is by all odds the ultimate source of who and what God is. There was no doubt in his mind that he was that source. He said that he is the Son of God, that everything he said and did was dictated by God. He said he is one with God the Father. He said, "Anyone who has seen me has seen the Father" (John 14:7).

Jesus also said, "I am the way and the truth and the life. No one comes to the Father except through me" (John 14:6). He could not have stated his claim to divinity more clearly.

I set out to determine, to my own satisfaction at least, if that claim was justified. Is Jesus who he said he is?

More is known – more books have been written — about Jesus, than almost any other person. The two largest categories in the Library of Congress are the Civil War and Jesus of Nazareth (*Y'shua — The Jewish Way to Say Jesus*, p. 33). What follows is a summary of facts and logic I have assembled dealing with the question of the divinity of Jesus.

Prophecies

From its first to its last book, the Old Testament of the Bible is a prelude leading to the New Testament. It is replete with prophecies of the coming of the Messiah (Christ). There appears to have been some room for confusion on one important aspect of the coming of Christ. Some prophets foresaw that the Christ would walk among them once as a suffering savior and then, after enough time for all people to have the opportunity of their free choice to be saved, to return as King. Others foresaw only his coming as a king, as a dictator to free Israel of foreign rule. Elements of each coming (advents) are found among Old Testament prophets.

The most interesting, informative and attractive presentation of principal Old Testament prophecies I have been able to find are in the book, *Y'shua — the Jewish Way to Say Jesus*. It is rich in Jewish tradition and history. Its author, Moishe Rosen, is retired chairman of the evangelical group called Jews for Jesus. Those who wish to probe this subject will want to read Mr. Rosen's book. Only bare bones are presented in what follows, and they owe much to that book.

— The Christ will be born in Bethlehem; his origins are from days of eternity (Micah 5:2).

— The Christ will be of the lineage of King David and eventually will rule from his throne. (Isaiah 9:6,7; Psalm 132:11).

— The Christ will be of virgin birth (Isaiah 7:14).

— The Christ will be preceded by the voice of one calling in the desert to make straight the way in the wilderness; the glory of the Lord will be revealed and all mankind will see it; then suddenly the Lord you are seeking will come (Isaiah 40:3-5; Malachi 3:1).

— The Christ will be a suffering savior. He will take up our infirmities and carry our sorrows; he will be pierced for our transgressions, crushed for our iniquities and by his wounds we shall be healed (Isaiah 53:4,5).

— The Christ will be betrayed by a close friend (Psalm 41:9). His betrayer will be rewarded with thirty pieces of silver (Zechariah 11:13).

— The Christ will be crucified. For a few moments he will take on every sin of man and cry out, "My God, My God, why have you forsaken me?" but he will triumph. He will be resurrected and all the family of nations will bow down before him (Psalm 22).

— The Christ will arrive 490 years after a prophecy by Daniel; his presence will come to an abrupt end before the Roman destruction of the Temple and of the entire city of Jerusalem (Daniel 9:24-26).

These dates correspond first to Jesus' entry into Jerusalem, and second to the year 70 A.D. when the Romans devastated Jerusalem and the Temple.

As the author of *Y'shua, the Jewish Way to Say Jesus* puts it, "If Jesus is not the Christ, who else of his generation was?"

Each of these prophecies — and many more like them — deserves commentary, but this is not a book about prophecies I will single out a few for comment.

How could Jesus of Nazareth be born in Bethlehem? The Gospels of the New Testament will tell us. In fewest words, a national census was being held and for it all families were ordered to return to the town of the father's birth. Thus, Joseph (husband of Mary, mother of Jesus) born in Bethlehem, but settled in Nazareth, made the journey and Jesus was born while they were still there.

As for virgin birth, which seems preposterous to many, C. S. Lewis has pointed out in his book, *Miracles— A Preliminary Study*, that surely the God who created us and designed the normal process by which we reproduce could, if he chose, have a different process easily at hand any time he wishes.

The voice of one calling in the desert was, of course, John the Baptist. As noted in the previous chapter, John specifically denied that he was the Christ, but declared that Jesus is.

The close friend who betrayed Jesus as a prerequisite to his crucifixion, was, of course, Judas Iscariot, one of his twelve disciples; he was paid thirty pieces of silver for his betrayal.

Most impressive for its detailed accuracy is David's prophecy of the crucifixion of Jesus in Psalm 22. Writing some thousand years before the actual event, the details of David's prophecy coincide in every way with the description of Jesus' crucifixion given in each of the four New Testament Gospels — so closely that they defy both coincidence and conspiracy. Even the action and speech of third parties are included in David's prophecy. The cross is unlikely even to have been known to David as an instrument of execution. Psalm 22 is brief and most interesting to read.

Miracles

Jesus was often taunted by representatives of the

Temple hierarchy to prove that he was the Son of God by performing some miraculous feat — presumably by making a mountain move or by ascending in the air to the top of a temple peak. He steadfastly criticized his questioners for lack of faith. He refused to be a part of such meaningless feats, saying he would be involved in but one miracle of such drama — his resurrection from the dead.

On the other hand, where compassion for the poor, the sick, the lame, the blind and the hungry was involved, Jesus would go out of his way to perform miraculous healing. The Gospels all tell of his intense compassion for those who suffered. And he preached to them on every occasion.

On the surface one of his miracles would appear to have been for his own convenience — walking on water. As told in the Gospels, Jesus and his disciples had been separated by huge crowds who had come to hear and be cured. Jesus had slipped away from a crowd to find rest in prayer; his disciples finally left by boat to reach the other side of the lake, away from the crowd.

When Jesus later looked for his disciples he saw them well out into the lake. He walked on the water out to their boat. It suggests that he chose to do so as part of preparing them to have enough faith in him to carry on after his return to his natural spiritual form. They were understandably impressed to the point of fear. Jesus called them down for their lack of faith.

Walking on water and the virgin birth of Jesus are the two miracles most often scoffed at, though the resurrection is the miracle that transcends them all (see below). The rationale for the walk on water is the same as for the virgin birth. If God has the power and knowledge to create the universe and maintain its order in part through gravity, why should it seem impossible for him to have another process or order at hand for any special occasion he chooses? God can do anything.

Logic

For many it may seem unreasonable on the part of Jesus, if he is God, that he did not prove himself by miraculous feats beyond human imagination. Why not thus avoid the cross and a need for resurrection? Such actions would have been completely out of God's character. Jesus, assuming he is who he said he was, came for the principal reason of dying on the cross, not to perform miraculous feats to avoid it. He said precisely that (John 10:17-18, 12:27).

God, if he chose, could at any time in history have forced us to recognize and accept that he is the one true God. He created the universe with humans, animals and all that are in it. He can do whatever he chooses. Obviously, God has never shown an interest in forcing us to accept him. To believers who come before him of their own will in love and worship, God gives of his grace with amazing abundance. But God insists , and always has, on faith in him by each believer.

I find particularly troubled those people of high intellect who for one reason or another have been led down false paths away from Jesus — by, the wrong teacher, convent, church — and, failing to find the true Christ, have felt rejected despite their intellect. They are tempted to try another form of religion or just to reject them all rather than to persevere and find the true Christ.

I must agree that the atheist cannot be proved wrong by a court of law or legal process; much less can a believer be proved wrong. On the surface the agnostic would seem to have advantages in a debate on these lines. There is the inherent appeal of intellectual snobbishness, of leaning back with no real effort on one's own part and saying, "Prove it; I'll accept nothing that can't be proved, nothing that is not clear to my intellect."

There's that attitude of being in an elite group, not of any group swayed by faith. Then, there are those who like to imagine that they are strong, silent types; for them, religion is for the weak. This may be a great feeling until inevitably we realize, and sometimes even acknowledge, that we can't make it on our own.

I am moved by the story told by Paul Harvey (a radio commentator and syndicated columnist). He told of a farmer who, in effect, remained a religious skeptic. One winter night, with his family at church, a blizzard blew in. He heard a thumping against his window. Small shivering birds were flying about desperately and, near blind by the snow, trying to gain shelter by flying through the lighted window. The farmer, who loved birds, opened the window, but the birds were too frightened of him to come in.

After desperate thinking, he put on his storm gear and, taking a lantern, ran out to a barn and threw its doors open. There was much warm hay in the barn and no wind or snow. Frantically, he tried to show the birds with his lantern and even to wave them into the safety of the barn. Fearing enclosed places, not trusting him, the birds would not enter. After a long effort and as the animals in the barn grew restless, he closed the barn and returned to his house. And the thought came to him, "Now I know why God had to come as one of us."

There is one attitude toward Jesus that I find that logic can expose as quite unsustainable. It is what C. S. Lewis called the "patronizing nonsense" that Jesus was a great human teacher; we love the beauty and the simplicity of what he taught, but he is not God. For Jesus to have stated with deadly earnest and every appearance of sanity that he was God, as Lewis put it, is quite simply the most shocking thing ever said by human lips.

Lewis goes on to write that either Jesus was everything he said he was or he was the greatest egomaniac, liar, and farce of all time, that Jesus left no middle ground about himself and that he intended it that way. He is either God in the person of the Son or he is of no interest at all. (*Mere Christianity,* p 45).

Timing

God possesses infinite wisdom, and we would expect him, if he chose to walk the earth in human form, to choose the perfect time. Jesus came at a time when the world was as near one world as it is ever likely to be. The Pax Romana assured legal order throughout the Roman Empire as never before or since. There was one language (Greek) commonly understood throughout that world (and the message was to be carried to all nations). Means of transportation were the best they had been in history with Roman roads spanning each country and with seaways open and frequently plied.

As a footnote about the then known manageable world, Eusebius wrote that tradition tells us that the apostles Bartholomew, Andrew, John, Mark as well as Peter and Paul carried the word to parts of Asia, Europe, and Africa. Bartholomew was reported to have spread the word in India (*The History of the Church*, 107, 213-14).

Resurrection

This is the big one. I explored it carefully. If Jesus was not dead, buried, yet risen in resurrected form, then all his claims of who he said he was come to nothing.

Jesus knew this. Indeed, he proclaimed the challenge facing him. After the Temple leaders had decided that Jesus was a danger to them and must be killed, these leaders sent some of their astute representatives to engage Jesus in debate on matters of religion and scripture. This was done before crowds for maximum effect. But on every test, Jesus had answers that neither the experts nor any in the crowd could dispute.

As a last resort the experts demanded of Jesus that, if he were God, he must show them some great sign, some miracle of which only God would be capable. Jesus, rebuking them for lack of faith, repeated that he would show but one such sign, that he would die at their hands, be buried and in three days arise from the dead alive — the resurrection.

Not surprisingly, the resurrection has been the subject of more scrutiny, scholarly investigation and exercises in logic than any aspect of the life of Jesus. Enough books have been written on it to fill a library. They range from eyewitness accounts to studies archaeological in nature to systematic recordings in summary of findings by the most serious scholars. Let us examine eyewitness accounts.

Gospel Accounts

Accounts of the death, burial and resurrection of Jesus are given in each of the four Gospels of the New Testament. Two of the Gospels are eyewitness accounts, written by disciples, later apostles, who formed a closely knit band that practically lived with Jesus during his ministry. One of them, Matthew, probably had the sharpest memory and quickest resort to note taking of them all. He had been a tax collector. The other eyewitness Gospel is that of John, who was in all probability the closest of any mortal to Jesus during his ministry. He was apparently a former disciple of John the Baptist.

A third Gospel, that of John Mark, is widely accepted as based on sermons by and conversations with Peter, who with John and James formed an inner council closest to Jesus. Mark, a youngster at the time of the ministry of Jesus, but probably a witness to its last days, became what we would call a secretary and traveling aid to Peter, later to others, and still later a major leader of the church.

The other Gospel was written by a Gentile, a physician called Luke. His is a work based on careful research during that crucial period when so many witnesses to the events in the life and resurrection of Jesus were easily accessible. And Luke, we are told by Eusebius, came to know as trusted sources the important figures surrounding Jesus. He later traveled extensively with Paul (below).

William Barclay has pointed out, as an example of the care for facts shown by Luke, that Luke dated the emergence of John the Baptist by no fewer than six contemporary notable events of the time.

The New York Times (11/8/99) in a book review of *DESIRE OF THE EVERLASTING HILLS –The World Before and After Jesus* by Thomas Cahill quotes the author's conclusion, which concerns the authors of the four Gospels:

"Yet the evangelists . . . who were not practiced writers of any sort, these four succeeded where almost all others failed. To a writer's eyes, this feat is a miracle just a little short of raising the dead."

To me it is such a miracle. As we shall see in subsequent pages, it is another miracle that Jesus foretold, for it was not the unlearned authors who inspired their words. It was the Holy Spirit within them.

What do these Gospels tell us about the resurrection? They have much to tell. And what they tell merits a careful and extended approach. First, they leave no room for doubt but that Jesus was killed on the cross. As a means of assessing the change in the disciples of Jesus from the moment of his arrest, trial, crucifixion and later, a brief review of these events is useful.

According to his disciples, Jesus had begun long before to tell them that, when his time came, he would be arrested, tried, and crucified, but that he would be resurrected from the dead on the third day. He had to do this gently but firmly, for he knew that the immediate reaction of even his most ardent disciples would be fear, then desertion of him in despair. He wanted to spare them feelings of guilt; he wanted them to overcome that despair and to deliver his gospel to all nations.

Still the disciples held to the hope that Jesus would in the end become ruler of Israel. Hadn't they seen multitudes acclaiming Jesus for his miraculous cures of the blind, the deaf, the lepers? Hadn't they heard that crowd proclaiming Jesus as son of David, mightiest and greatest ruler in Israel's history? True, each time such crowds called out for him to become their king and for him to conquer the world for Israel, Jesus withdrew from their presence. But the disciples held to their dream.

The message of his true destiny should not have shocked Jesus' disciples. They had heard him teaching the crowds to love their enemies and pray for those who persecute them, to seek first the kingdom of God, that he (Jesus) had come as a ransom for the many, to render to Caesar that which is Caesar's, and a whole philosophy contrary to a conquering, warlike king. The disciples were devout and loyal learners. They were anything but sophisticated, being essentially fishermen, a tax collector, and a couple of reformed revolutionists.

When Jesus was seized by a large detachment of armed Roman soldiers led by Temple officials and police, it came as no surprise to him. He had done his best to prepare his disciples for how, when and where it would happen. He identified himself to the arresting band with no resistance, asking only that his disciples be free to go their way unharmed.

And that they did. Let the reader try to picture the scene. Neither Jesus nor his disciples had slept for many hours. It was night. The armed band carried many flaring torches. They also carried with them an atmosphere of ruthless cruelty difficult to imagine in present times, as is death by crucifixion. These are all elements that incite fear just as hard rapping on a door in the middle of the night by an armed band of the Gestapo would later do.

When Jesus had told his disciples that in the frightening chaos of his arrest and trial they would temporarily abandon him, Peter, rash and impulsive almost once too often, insisted that he would never desert his Lord. Jesus, with compassion, told him that before the rooster crowed that very day, Peter would deny him three times.

And so it happened. Such was the atmosphere of fear that in the course of the trial of Jesus, while waiting outside among palace guards and in response to charges, Peter three times denied that he even knew Jesus. The rooster crowed and Peter, seized with the enormity of his failure, ran outside and wept bitterly. To his everlasting credit, he swallowed his pride, rejoined his fellow disciples and did not try to conceal his failure.

Mark, author of the gospel that bears his name, had a rare gift for color, and it appears briefly in his account of that night. He was hardly more than a boy, but his parents were committed to Jesus — indeed, it was probably at their house that Jesus and the disciples gathered. Apparently Mark could not resist secretly following Jesus as he left the house of his parents and ascended Mount of Olives to the Garden of Gethsemane, where he overheard Jesus say he would be arrested. Mark's account of those events includes these apparently unnecessary sentences: "A young man, wearing nothing but a linen garment was following Jesus. When they seized him he fled naked leaving his garment behind" (Mark 14:51,52). It is clear to me that he was talking about himself.

The disciples remained clustered together, probably in the upper room of Mark's parents. All the assurances Jesus had given them that he would return seemed remote. They prayed for their own lives.

This much I found easy to envisage, but to fully comprehend the enormity of what was about to happen, I needed to learn more about crucifixion. Jesus walked willingly into it; his disciples were initially frightened out of their senses at the threat of being pulled into it.

Crucifixion

Every Jewish person of Jesus' day knew about crucifixion from childhood. It was always public, usually imposed by Roman soldiers on insurrectionists. An example – an opportunity to view its horror — was by calculation imposed on everyone. The description given here is taken from Professor Barclay's commentary on the Gospels of John and Matthew.

Barclay quotes Cicero describing crucifixion as the most horrible torture, incapable of description (Barclay on Matthew 27:27-31 and on John 19:17-22).

Crucifixion was always preceded by scourging. In this, a man was tied to a whipping post in such a way that his back was fully exposed. The lash with which he was whipped was a long leather thong studded at intervals with pellets of lead and sharpened pieces of bone. It literally tore the back into strips of flesh. Few remained conscious to the end; some died; many went raving mad. Jesus withstood all that.

The rest of the process is generally known. The subject, bleeding profusely from the scourging, was made to carry his cross to a hill outside the city by the longest route, so that he would be seen by as many as possible. He was nailed to the cross and left hanging until he died, from loss of blood, pain, shock, thirst — whatever it took. There were no survivors.

Thus it happened to Jesus. The Gospel accounts

tell that Jesus hung on the cross for six hours before he died. All of them tell that at the moment of death there was a great shout from Jesus. John, who wrote that he was standing close at hand, tells us the final word shouted was the Greek equivalent of "Finished!" As Barclay puts it, a victor's shout of triumph.

As the day's end was near, one of the soldiers pierced Jesus' side with a spear to be certain he was dead. The process of the crucifixion is such that it is only reasonable to accept that Jesus died on the cross. (Note below Pilate's reaction to the request for the dead body of Jesus.) What of the resurrection? But, first, I need to look more clearly at the burial.

The Empty Tomb

Two factors combine to make the tomb in which Jesus was buried relevant to the resurrection. First, in the Palestine of those days the tomb of any corpse was of great importance. The climate and, most important, the absence of any embalming method effective over more than a day or two made a solid, airtight tomb highly desirable. Such a tomb would usually be a cave of some size in solid rock around the front of which rugged grooves were made. Into these grooves a neatly fitting heavy stone was rolled into place after burial.

The second factor is that among the followers of Jesus were two men of wealth and position in the Temple establishment, Joseph of Arimathea and Nicodemus. Though they were unable to prevent the persecution of Jesus, they were determined to provide him with the best tomb they could find on short notice.

This they did. Immediately following the death of Jesus, Joseph "boldly" hurried to Pilate, then Governor of Judea, and requested the dead body of Jesus. Pilate, after verifying with the centurion that Jesus was indeed dead, complied (Mark 15:44-45). Joseph and Nicodemus wrapped the body of Jesus with spices and herbs and with strips of linen, in accordance with Jewish burial custom. They had the heavy stone rolled back into its grooves and left Jesus in the tomb.

Joseph and Nicodemus weren't the only ones to go to Pilate concerning burial arrangements for Jesus. The chief priest and others high in the Temple establishment went to inform Pilate that, while alive, Jesus had foretold that after his crucifixion he would rise in resurrected form on the third day. They expressed concern that in order to lend credence to this resurrection some of the disciples of Jesus might try to steal and hide the body of Jesus. They asked for and received assurances that a detachment of Roman guards would be stationed at the tomb to prevent any such effort. (The above is taken from accounts in each of the Gospels: Matthew 27:57-61, Mark 15:42-47, Luke 23:50-56, John 19:38-42.)

Resurrection Discovered

Now it is time for me to turn my attention fully to the central act, the focal point of Christianity. It was by the women followers of Jesus that the empty tomb was found and his resurrected person first seen. There had always been women followers of Jesus, including his mother. The culture of the time did not permit women anything like the status of apostle; they performed menial and essential tasks for Jesus and for those who could be apostles. The appeal of Jesus for them was enhanced precisely because he treated them with respect, even in that time and in that part of the world.

So it was that one of them arrived at the tomb where Jesus had been placed after his death. She arrived at sunrise on Sunday. (Jesus had died late Friday; nothing could have been done beyond a quick burial before the Sabbath, which began Friday evening.) She found only the empty tomb. Jesus appeared to her outside of the tomb in a physical form that seemed different from that of pre-resurrection. Only when he spoke her name did she recognize him. He told her to go tell the disciples what she had seen. This she quickly did. On being informed, Peter and John, leaving the others in the hidden room, raced to the site of the tomb and found it empty.

Thus to the evidence concerning the resurrection: the empty tomb. This is of central importance. Every plausible explanation of whether and how the tomb became empty deserves at least summary exploration.

Could it be that Jesus faked the whole thing? Could it be that he let himself be crucified, pierced by the spear, and buried? Could he then have awakened, say, from some deep swoon, pushed aside the stone too heavy for any ordinary man to move and

Jesus of Nazareth

walked away to the dismay of the startled and helpless Roman guards who probably would be executed for such an offense? To ask such questions is to answer them. Jesus had not eaten for days; he was tightly wrapped in grave clothes; he had lost most of the blood from his body. And where would he go to hide, walking on pierced feet with old wounds opening with every step?

And why go through with the crucifixion when he could so easily have avoided it by walking in the night back to the hills of Galilee or beyond before the guards seized him — as he predicted they would? Jesus had clear warning that his crucifixion was at hand. His disciples had urged him not to return to Jerusalem. Even a few Pharisees had warned him to stay away from Jerusalem. And wouldn't the Holy Spirit have let him know and helped prepare him for his destiny? Jesus persisted in his ministry in Jerusalem. The Jews — even that minority ruling the Temple — did not bring on the crucifixion of Jesus. He did.

Could the Jewish authorities have removed the body to prevent the tomb from becoming a site for mobilized efforts to make a martyr of Jesus? If so, would they not have promptly produced the body when Christianity began to spread so quickly in Jerusalem? Indeed, as the apostles spoke in Jerusalem and elsewhere with unceasing boldness and effectiveness, insisting that Jesus is Lord, and that they were witnesses to his resurrection from the dead, this was the urgent moment for the authorities to come forward with the dead body of Jesus and put an end to

Christianity (and riots in Jerusalem) once and for all. They did not. They fell back on the only weapon they had. They persecuted the apostles and expelled from the synagogue all who accepted Jesus as Lord.

Could the disciples of Jesus have overpowered the armed Roman guards, removed the sealed stone and made away with the body so that they could later claim that Jesus had risen on his own? But the disciples were reduced to a small band of terrorized and demoralized people. Moreover, would not such an event, with the bodies of dead Roman guards strewn about the place, have touched off a thorough house-to-house search by Romans and Jews? And would not such a theft have been made public by the chief priest and others of the Temple establishment? No such alarm was ever reported.

The Reaction of People

Richard Swinburne, professor of philosophy at Oxford, has applied and presented to an audience of more than one hundred philosophers convened at Yale an elaborate and intricate formula known as Bayes's theorem as a test of the probability of the resurrection of Jesus. Results were reassuring, a 97% probability (NYT 5/11/02). I'm not surprised. Using only such common sense as I have, I'm 100% persuaded simply by the reaction of people immediately after the event down to today. In the next pages I'll explain why.

And what gain would any such subterfuge have produced for the followers of Jesus? The strongest evidence for the resurrection of Jesus lies in the reaction of the people to that fact — reactions by his disciples in that period immediately following his crucifixion and reactions among countless others persecuted cruelly and ruthlessly for centuries thereafter, in some parts, even now.

For all those converted by the disciples, there was immediate excommunication from the synagogue which meant social ostracism, no work and more. In fact they were — and knew well that they were — in for lives of constant harassment and persecution. In the end most were either stoned to death or crucified. Only one apostle is known to have escaped violent death by persecution — the Apostle John, who died a very old man exiled, sentenced to hard labor, still writing and preaching that Jesus is the resurrected Christ. He kept writing.

Barclay put it well when he wrote that men do not endure martyrdom for impostors.

There remains then the most plausible explanation for the empty tomb. That it all happened just as the Gospel accounts say, that Jesus, being the Christ he always said he is, arose just as he said he would, and left the tomb only to materialize at will in resurrected form.

Post-resurrection Appearances

Over the next forty days Jesus appeared in his resurrected form on ten different occasions including to over 500 people at the same time, most of them still living when much of the New Testament was written (I Corinthians 15:6). On one occasion, when he first appeared to his disciples, the disciple Thomas was not present. Those present were overjoyed. Jesus told them to remain in hiding; he would join them later. When all this was excitedly related to Thomas, he refused to believe that Jesus was resurrected, saying he would do so only when he had seen and felt the wounded hands and pierced side of the resurrected body. Jesus later appeared to them all and invited Thomas to feel his wounds. After doing so the doubting Thomas was convinced, with much emotion (John 20:26-28).

I find it interesting that Jesus did not choose to appear in his resurrected form to masses of people, or at the Temple itself to erase any doubt of his resurrection. It is an instructive point to consider, along with the refusal of Jesus to demonstrate beyond doubt that he was (is) the Son of God before the crucifixion — he just said that he would perform but one miraculous proof and that was his resurrection.

The point is that God insists that faith, not legal proof, be the basis of worshiping him. It is a point that has been made earlier and will come up later in this book; it is both pervasive and essential.

So it is that Jesus appeared in his resurrected form only to those who believed in him. He made one exception: his brother James and his other brothers.

During his ministry his brothers had taken Jesus lightly, possibly even considering him to be under serious delusions. It's not hard to see why this would be so. They had watched their oldest brother grow from childhood to become head of the carpenter shop their father had left. They had probably been schooled in the skills of carpentry by Jesus. They had seen that Jesus was exceptional, astonishing even advanced teachers of scripture with his knowledge of it. But their brother! The Son of God! The long awaited Messiah! It was too much for them, although not too much for their mother.

Luke, in the book of Acts, tells us that Jesus appeared to his oldest brother, James. Both James and another brother, Jude, are authors of epistles that appear in the New Testament. Before the end of this post-resurrection period the gathering of Jesus' followers included "Mary the mother of Jesus, and his brothers" (Acts 1:14).

Much of this period was spent by Jesus in teaching his appointed disciples (now designated apostles) and preparing them for the work and suffering that awaited them. He breathed into the mouth of each and told them they had thus received the Holy Spirit. He promised them that soon after his departure the Holy Spirit would come into them in fullness and that upon that occasion all things would be clear to them. They would have great powers; the Spirit would tell them what to say whenever they were charged with blasphemy in his name; they need fear no one; he, himself would always be with them.

At the end of this final period, according to the Gospels and the book of Acts, Jesus led his followers outside of Jerusalem. He told them to wait for the gift of the Holy Spirit in his fullness and then, "You will be my witnesses in Jerusalem, and in all Judea and Samaria and to the ends of the earth (Acts 1:8).

He then ascended into clouds, returning to his eternal spiritual state.

The followers of Jesus returned to their locked room and awaited further events in high spirits, praying and singing hymns. On the day of Pentecost there was suddenly a sound like the blowing of a violent wind into the room; they saw what seemed to be tongues of fire that separated and came to rest on each of them; all of them were filled with the Holy Spirit, never to be the same.

More on the Reaction of the People

One of the first things the disciples noticed was an ability to speak foreign languages they had never known before. On the occasion of Pentecost there were in Jerusalem many Jews visiting from foreign lands. On hearing and recognizing the languages native to them, they were amazed; the followers of Jesus were even accused of being drunk, because of their high spirits and the foreign tongues.

Peter, who had taken charge as leader and spokesman for the group, went out to the crowd, raised his voice and delivered the first Christian sermon. Though it came from the mouth of an ordinary fisherman (before he met Jesus) it is as eloquent and complete as one could hear from the best educated minister of today. It is found in Luke's book of Acts 2:24-39. Luke reports that those who accepted the sermon were baptized and about three thousand were added to the followers of Jesus that day.

Could this be the same Peter that had three

times, to his utter desolation, denied the man he considered Lord God? It was, and this was only the beginning of the dramatic changes in the followers of Jesus which serve to substantiate the resurrection of their Lord.

Led by Peter and John, increasing numbers of the followers of Jesus were emboldened not only to come out from their hidden quarters but to appear and speak out each afternoon during prayers at the Temple itself. On one such occasion they passed at the entrance a crippled beggar who looked to Peter and John for money. Peter commanded that the lame man look straight at John and him and said, "Silver or gold I do not have, but what I have I give you. In the name of Jesus Christ of Nazareth walk." The man rose to his feet and walked for the first time in his life (Acts 3:6).

The people present for Temple prayers, and long familiar with the formerly lame man's condition, were amazed and crowded around Peter and John. Peter seized the occasion to deliver a speech to them: Jesus of Nazareth was the long awaited Messiah; he had been crucified, was dead and buried; Peter was witness to his resurrection and his return to God the Father.

The priests and the captain of the temple guard heard Peter and were greatly disturbed. Peter and John were jailed overnight and brought before the high priest and elders of the Temple who asked by what power or what name they had done what they had done.

The once cowed Peter let loose with a bold and

elegant reply. Among other things, he told the high court that "It is by the name of Jesus Christ of Nazareth . . . Salvation is found in no one else, for there is no other name under heaven given to men by which we must be saved" (Acts 4:9-12).

Luke goes on to tell us the officials of the highest Jewish council (the Sanhedrin) realized that Peter and John were unschooled, ordinary men of great courage. They commanded Peter and John not to speak or teach anywhere in the name of Jesus. But Peter and John answered, "Judge for yourselves whether it is right in God's sight to obey you rather than God. For we cannot help speaking about what we have seen and heard" (Acts 4:19,20). After further threats the Sanhedrin let Peter and John go.

Persecution Spreads

I wanted to know what happened to the Apostles, but I discovered that apart from the New Testament we do not possess details of the further events in the lives of most of the followers of Jesus. Barclay attributes this in part to the style of writing history among the Jews of that day and partly to the plausible assumption that much of what was written has been lost. Some of the leaders in the early Christian era had the forethought to gather all information they could from eyewitnesses still alive and put it in writing, some of which directly or indirectly still survives. These include writings of Papias and Polycarp, born in the years 60 and 69 A.D. Also, Eusebius (A.D. 263-339), a Greek Christian born and educated in Palestine where he later was a bishop, wrote voluminously of information available in scrolls written much earlier but then available along with what he could learn on his own. Volumes of his writings are available today.

Eusebius wrote that Peter traveled with his wife (who served Jesus from the early years of his ministry) and preached the Gospel of Jesus in Jerusalem and other parts of Palestine and in Pontus, Galatia, Bithynia, Cappadocia, over much of Asia Minor before he finally settled in Rome as Bishop. The writings of Clement, an early bishop quoted by Eusebius, tell of the death by persecution of Peter's wife as Peter called encouragement to her, saying, "Remember the Lord!" Eusebius also tells us from oral history that Peter was crucified in Rome with his head toward the ground, at his request, insisting that he was not worthy to die in the exact way of his Lord.

John, as predicted by Jesus, was to outlive all other apostles, serving for some years in exile at hard labor on the island of Patmos until a less punitive Roman became emperor. When John was released he resumed his service as bishop at Ephesus (Asia Minor), where he died and was buried.

As the apostles spread the word, disciples and followers grew in number and expanded geographically, as Jesus had instructed. They also became known as the Church, sometimes called the Way. They had always needed organization. Among other things, those recognized as members were unable to find work, for they were thrown out of the synagogue. Such matters as procurement or food, lodging and drink became a problem the moment they were emboldened to spread the word of Jesus publicly. Peter and John had naturally assumed the role as leaders. When James, "the brother of the Lord," joined their ranks, Peter and John deferred to him.

James was a strong and devout leader, known by the title, James the Righteous. He was named Bishop of Jerusalem, the first bishop. Peter and John, while making missionary trips from time to time, joined James to form the Council of Jerusalem.

Stephen, who was to become the first martyr after Jesus, was a Grecian Jew who had become a follower of Jesus early and was particularly well liked by his colleagues. He appeared often in the Synagogue of Freedmen (Jews largely not of Israel). Opposition among non-Christian Jews arose against Stephen spurred by his successes. Attempts were made to contest Stephen's proclamations but, to the increasing chagrin of his opposition, Stephen invariably justified himself. As losers sometimes do, they began to plot how to do away with Stephen. They secretly circulated word that Stephen was speaking words of blasphemy against Moses and God.

Stephen was brought before the Sanhedrin for investigation. He explained himself in a long and inspired discourse, giving a history of the Jewish people and their relationship with God and his prophets. Stephen ended with these words,

"Was there ever a prophet your fathers did not persecute? They even killed those who predicted the coming of the Righteous One. And now you have betrayed and murdered him — you have received the law . . . but you have not obeyed it" (Acts 7:52,53).

He must have known he was asking for it. He must have reckoned it was worth it.

Members of the Sanhedrin were furious. They dragged Stephen out of the city and stoned him to death, the ultimate penalty a Jew could impose on another. While they were stoning him, Stephen called out, "Lord Jesus, receive my spirit." He fell to his knees and cried out, "Lord, do not hold this sin against them," and died (Acts 7:59-60).

Saul of Tarsus

Overseeing, quite possibly instigating, the stoning of Stephen was a Pharisee, Saul of Tarsus. The stories of all the disciples are moving and inspiring, but to me the story of Saul stands out even more than the others as proof of Jesus' divinity. Saul was young, ardent, ambitious, one of the most promising scholars of the Law. His education was the best that could be received. He described himself as a Hebrew born of Hebrews, a Pharisee and son of a Pharisee. His father had won Roman citizenship with all its privileges; Saul had inherited it from him.

Saul had a passion for the Law, which he saw, at that time, as the only vehicle by which to be true to God. He saw in Jesus and his followers the complete contradiction of everything he had staked his most promising career and life on.

The Messiah, when he came, insisted Saul, would be nothing like Jesus; he would be the militaristic conqueror of the world on behalf of the

Jewish nation. Saul led the way among Temple leaders in rage and bitter hostility against Jesus and those who believed in him. For, if Jesus was right, everything Saul had dedicated himself to and prospered in was dead wrong.

Saul noted that, as Stephen died, there had been on his face a look of peace that Saul had never experienced. He redoubled his efforts to persecute every follower of Jesus, with authority and encouragement from the Temple crowd. To his chagrin this only resulted in dispersing the apostles to other parts of Israel, where thy converted new and larger crowds to Jesus. Saul began a systematic campaign to destroy the church in Jerusalem, going from house to house and dragging men and women into prison. Saul then went to the high priest and obtained from him letters to the synagogues in Damascus so that if he found any Christians there, he could take them, men and women, as prisoners to Jerusalem.

On his way to Damascus, accompanied by others under him, Saul had a personal experience that would be impossible ever to forget. As Saul was later to relate many times, on nearing Damascus, a light suddenly flashed down on him from above. Saul fell to the ground and heard a voice saying, "Saul, Saul why do you persecute me?" Saul asked, "Who are you, Lord?" He was told, "I am Jesus," and was instructed to go into the city where he would be told what to do.

When he attempted to get up, Saul found that he was blind. For three days he was blind. Then one of the followers of Jesus came to him and said that Jesus had sent him so that Saul might see again and be filled with the Holy Spirit. Saul's sight was restored immediately and he was baptized (Acts 9:1-2).

Jesus wanted Saul's attention. He got it.

Thus when Saul began appearing in the synagogues, where he was expected to demand help in ruthlessly rooting out every man and woman who was a believer in Jesus as the Christ, he amazed his listeners by preaching the Gospel that Jesus is Lord.

I've found Paul's epistles a key to understanding Christianity. Admittedly, he sometimes riles, even exasperates me. He asks much, and I'm prompted to think, "Who are you to insist I live your way?" But then I remember that Jesus knew how Paul would write and chose him and the Holy Spirit inspired his work. Then, too, Paul wrote more about God's grace than any Biblical writer.

To me, Paul is essential. And there are times, for example, in his epistles to the Philippians and to the Colossians, both written while he was in prison, when his words soar with inspired beauty. Paul's epistle to the Romans, especially the first eight chapters, is to me one of the greatest, perhaps the greatest, writing on Christian theology. If left alone on a deserted island with a choice of only two books, I'd want John and Romans.

Jesus wanted Saul's intellect, zeal and fervor to carry his Gospel to all parts of the then known world. He wanted Saul to be tireless and effective as a missionary and theologian all in one. In keeping with his conversion and the work of the Lord within him, Saul considered himself a new creation. In part, it is thought, for this reason he changed his name to Paul. He counted himself an apostle on grounds that he had seen and conversed with Jesus. He preached the Gospel in Israel, but especially in foreign parts — Asia Minor, Cyprus and Crete, Greece and Macedonia and, finally, in Rome, the center of world power. His determination to spread the Word to foreign parts also probably led to changing his name to Paul, which is Greek for the Hebrew Saul. Paul's letters (epistles) to the churches he had founded, or helped to found, make up today a large segment of the New Testament.

If we accept, first, that Jesus was God incarnate and, second, that the spreading of Christianity was the turning point in the history of humankind, then it seems to me that Paul was the most important human being in the history of the world.

Paul paid a price, but it was a price that he never regretted. Wherever he went, two things seemed sure to happen: a body of believers would be converted and would form a new church, and Paul would be chased out of the city by nonbelievers, after being beaten, threatened, stoned and left for dead, at times imprisoned.

Paul lists his hardships in one of his letters to the church in Corinth:

"I have been in prison . . . been flogged more severely, and been exposed to death again and again. Five times I received from the Jews the forty lashes minus one. Three times I was beaten with rods, once I was stoned, three times I was shipwrecked . . . I have been in danger from rivers, in danger from bandits, in danger from my own countrymen, in danger from Gentiles; in danger in the city, in danger in the country, in danger at sea; and in danger from false brothers . . . I have known hunger and thirst" (II Corinthians 11:23-27).

He had witnesses ready and willing to support every claim. From his prison in Rome Paul was able to write,

> "I have learned to be content whatever the circumstances. I know what it is to be in need, and I know what it is to have plenty. I have learned the secret of being content in any and every situation. . . . . I can do anything through him who gives me strength" (Philippians 4:11-13).

To satisfy the depravity of Nero, as the empire was falling, Paul was beheaded in Rome. (Being a Roman citizen, he could not be crucified.)

Why would a man like Paul who had family, position, and a future that promised ease and comfort throw it all away and adopt the life he did if Jesus of Nazareth was just a wise teacher? The wisdom of Jesus' teaching had left Saul cold; it was what the Spirit of the living Jesus Christ can do inside a person that set Saul of Tarsus on fire.

Others

There were others who became as fearless and

faithful as Paul. James, brother of John, was the first of the apostles to be killed by persecution as he spread the word. The Apostle Philip followed the same path. Indeed, there is every reason to believe that, as Jesus implied would happen, all of the apostles of Jesus but John met death by persecution. Eusebius tells us that James, the brother of Jesus, was stoned and clubbed to death for proclaiming the divinity of Jesus.

We shall never know the full number of people who sacrificed themselves to death by persecution to spread the Gospel of Jesus and his word. In an appendix to his *"History of the Church,"* Eusebius lists prominent leaders of Christianity who were martyred by Roman emperors. Some entries had to be reduced to, "Many eminent men," "An alarming number," etc.

Yet in little more that thirty years Christianity, which began in a small corner of Palestine, reached Rome and began flourishing there and in most of Asia Minor, in Athens, and Alexandria, and even farther afield. As Barclay wrote in his commentary on John 17:6-8,

"When Jesus left this world he did not seem to have great grounds for hope. He seemed to have achieved so little and to have won so few, and it was the great and the orthodox and the religious of the day who had turned against him. But Jesus . . . was not afraid of small beginnings . . . He seemed to say, Give me these eleven ordinary men and I will change the world."

Whenever the emperor of the Roman Empire

was relatively tolerant, Christianity flourished. Slaves constituted a huge part of the population and included many professional men. They did not exist in the eyes of Roman law and were generally so treated except by Christians. Slaves were especially receptive to Jesus. Some of high position in the emperor's court were converted.

When the emperor was intolerant, corrupt and cruel, Christians dug in and submitted in large numbers to death by incredibly cruel means. A trap that led to particularly large numbers of deaths by persecution was the order that everyone in the empire must on regular occasions proclaim publicly that Caesar is god. The Christians refused to pay lip service and paid the price.

Missionaries around the world to this day live in extreme hardship often facing death in proclaiming Jesus of Nazareth as Lord, God the Son.

A. M. Rosenthal wrote a column that often appeared opposite the editorial page of *The New York Times*. In his column of May 13, 1997, he wrote, "... in China and other communist countries and in at least eight Muslim countries Christians are arrested, beaten, tortured or killed for their Christianity." He urged Americans to take action against such practices.

Pastors all over this country give up financially promising opportunities and, unlike the rare evangelists whose exposed wealth makes the evening news, follow a poorly paid career of great demands on them and their families to make the same proclamation.

Today there are in the world an estimated two

billion persons professing their Christianity (estimated at 1.8 billion in 1990 by David Barrett and Todd Johnson and extrapolated to roughly two billion in *Our Globe and How to Reach It*).

Why so much sacrifice, even surrendering to extreme cruelty, by so many? Why the persistent growth over some 2,000 years in the number of those professing that Jesus is God the Son and laying their lives on the line, committing themselves to him?

Conclusion

The answer, surely, is that Jesus is everything he said he is and for this reason was resurrected from death by crucifixion, leaving an empty tomb.

As Barclay put it,

> He (Jesus) was not one who lived nobly and died gallantly for a lost cause; he was one whose claims were vindicated by the fact that he rose again (commentary on John 6:59-65).

I examine some of the implications of accepting Jesus as God the Son in what follows. Once again, however, I urge the reader not to leave this fundamental question unanswered in his or her mind. Think it through! Is Jesus who he said he is?

CHAPTER VI

Implications

※

Once Jesus is fully accepted as God in the person of the Son, implications of enormous importance follow. First, we want to learn all we can about him and what he taught, to read the Gospels, and more.

One general conclusion is this: God is not only of infinite power, infinite wisdom and holiness, he is love; he cares deeply about the human race. There are no apparent reasons why God should be bothered if the human race he created and presented with a free will chooses to adopt morals repulsive to him, to be constantly at war among and within themselves, and to be miserable and making a mess of things generally.

God's Love – Our Love

But he WAS bothered. And he acted. He had

known what would be needed at the latest since rebellion against his will by Adam and Eve. His plan to send a part of himself to live and to walk among us as a suffering savior runs through the Old Testament, beginning with its first book.

He acted in a most startling way that changed the course of human history. He came, in the form of his son, had himself born as a babe into an ordinary, but holy family, and walked among us, showing us by his action and teaching how to live. Of great importance, God the Son told us and showed us what God the Father is really like.

The fact that he came selflessly to help the human race, the message of his ministry (see following chapter), the way he allowed himself to die, all point to a simple conclusion: God is love. And he is full of grace, which comprises the unmerited gifts of God to humankind and to individuals, an essential aid to growth in him.

We can never win the favor of God, never earn it, never buy it. It is his gift to us; it is unmerited, it is given freely, but only by grace through faith. This is hard for us to accept — that we just turn loose, have faith, and God takes over.

But, it's his way.

The apostle John wrote in his first epistle, "We love, because he first loved us" (I John 4:19). God's love is unconditional. He loves us, each individual, from the beginning to the end of our physical lives, always wanting what his infinite wisdom and holiness tell him is best for us — all of the time: when we sin; when we curse him; what is worse, when we

Implications

---

ignore him; no matter who we are or what we do. He sees the maximum potential for good in each of us — however deeply buried — right up to the end of life as we know it. Then, of course, there must be judgment, about which more later.

What is the basis for these claims of God's unconditional love? The cross on which Jesus was crucified is the most graphic for all to see and sufficient evidence in itself. The hours of excruciating pain and attempted humiliation of Jesus — man's ultimate inhumanity to man — had been anticipated. The crucifixion of the Son of God had been foretold and described in incredible detail, for example, some one thousand years earlier by David in Psalm 22 (see Prophecies). God knew well the consequences. Jesus came and lived among us to die on the cross. At the height of his pain he was able to look upon all those who had scourged him, beaten him, nailed him to the cross and tormented him and ask that God forgive them.

Our Love for Others

In Greek, the language in which the New Testament was written, there are different words for love — for example, a word for passionate, sexual love, and a word for warm affection within a family. Writers of the New Testament, in describing the love of God and the love that Jesus taught that we all should have for one another, chose an unusual Greek word and made it their own. That word is agapé. Barclay gave a meaning of this in his commentary on Ephesians 4:1-3: nothing anyone does will make us want anything but whatever in God's judgment may be their highest good.

John Wesley, the great English evangelist whose life spanned the eighteenth century, used less emotional terms, calling for a sincere, tender and disinterested love for all mankind (*The Burning Heart*, p. 244). Albert Outler, in *Theology in the Wesleyan Spirit*, quotes Wesley as urging that we love of God and love every man (p. 83).

Agapé love does not insist that we must admire or even like an Adolph Hitler or Joseph Stalin. It is by all accounts a love that always sees the best potential and wants that best for everyone. It is an unconditional love.

Jesus taught that God's love was like that of a father. He referred to God, by literal translation, as his "Dad" or "Daddy," (*Abba*), as if to impress that we are helpless children utterly dependent on him whether we realize it or not.

The Prodigal Son

Jesus often made his points through parables. I find his parable on the loving father (God) — known more widely as the "Prodigal Son" — especially lovely and fitting to God's love and forgiving grace. In summary, and paraphrased, it goes like this, based on Luke 15:11-24:

There was a man with two sons. The younger one asked to be given his share of the estate now. The father complied, dividing his estate between his

Implications

two sons. The younger son set off for distant lands where he squandered his wealth in wild living. He became so much in need that he had to take work from a man who sent him into the fields to feed his pigs, yet he was not himself given even what the pigs had to eat.

When the young son was near starvation, he remembered how well-fed and treated were those hired by his father. He made up his mind that he would return to his father, memorizing as he trudged back home the speech he would make: "Father, I have sinned against heaven and against you; I am no longer worthy to be called your son; make me like one of your hired men." But while the young son was still a long way off, his father saw him and was filled with compassion. Running to his son, he threw his arms around him and kissed him. The son made his speech in humility. The father sent for fresh robes, a ring and sandals for his son and ordered that the fatted calf be killed to have a feast and celebrate, saying this son of mine was dead and is alive again; he was lost and is found.

I am touched that the father was looking down the road for his son, implying a habit, and by the gracious and loving forgiveness of the father, the misdeeds of the son were as though they had never happened. But note, also, that the son returned in repentance, deeply sorry that he had sinned against his father, dedicated to a complete change in his life, asking forgiveness and the privilege of working as a hired man. We are that son or daughter; God is the father.

The need to have faith in God's unconditional

love, his forgiveness of penitent, confessed sin as though the sin never happened is the basis of a contemporary story. It is told of a small church where among the congregation there were an elderly lady who was known as one who in prayer actually conversed with — not just listened to — God, and a young man who had committed a sin he felt was too great for God ever to forgive though he earnestly prayed for it. On learning of the lady's great gift, the young man lost no time in explaining his situation to her and asking if she would ask God if he had been forgiven. She said she would. When next they met, the conversation went as follows:

> "Did you ask him?"
> "Yes."
> "What'd he say? Did he forgive me or is it hopeless?"
> "He said he couldn't remember."

And take heart! In the sentence immediately before the parable on the prodigal son Luke quotes Jesus saying, "There is rejoicing in the presence of the angels of God over one sinner who repents." (Luke 15:10). In his commentary on Ephesians 1:1-2, Barclay gives us these verses:

> How Thou canst think so well of us,
> And be the God Thou art,
> Is darkness to my intellect,
> But sunshine to my heart.

Implications

The Kingdom of God and His Will

The kingdom of God exists wherever anyone lives exclusively by the will of God. It's easy to see how this would be the case in a heavenly hereafter. But, as Professor Barclay (and, far earlier, Martin Luther) pointed out in his commentary on Matthew 6:10, Jesus gave us the explanation of the kingdom of God in one short sentence. At the request of some of his disciples, Jesus gave them an example of how to pray, commonly known as the Lord's Prayer. The sentence on the kingdom of God is, "Your [God's] kingdom come, your will be done on earth as it is in heaven." The kingdom of God is, then, ours now and always when we live by God's will.

As C. S. Lewis wrote, "Aim at Heaven and you will get earth thrown in; aim at the earth and you will get neither" (*Mere Christianity*, p. 113).

Why should living exclusively by the will of God be heavenly? The rationale of it for those who have read this far is simple; the realization of it is something else. Of central importance, we must bear in mind that God is love; he loves and cares deeply that each one of us has the opportunity to be saved — to find his kingdom. Thus we have the cross.

In the next chapter we shall look into what is God's will for us, based on what Jesus taught.

CHAPTER VII

What Jesus Taught

∞

The best source for learning what Jesus taught is the New Testament, specifically its four Gospels. The summary that follows falls into two parts, statements on the kingdom of God and statements on how to find it. The reader may recall that one definition of the kingdom of God was given at the end of the previous chapter.

The Kingdom of God

I have been struck by the importance Jesus attached to this. When we read in Luke 4:43, "I must preach the good news of the kingdom of God to the other towns also, because that is why I was sent. . . ." What did he have in mind? As I delved deeper, I learned that the kingdom of God — often used interchangeably with the kingdom of heaven — and its meaning have always attracted Christian theologians.

Most assume easily enough that there is a heavenly state of existence after death for those who die in Christ. What surprised me is that its very simplicity causes many, including some of the greatest minds, to miss the point.

Yet many others of great intellect have studied the Bible and come to embrace it. They include, to mention only a few and not those already listed in the chapter on creation, Augustine of Hippo, Blaise Pascal, John Bunyan, Erasmus, Fyodor Dostoevsky, Goethe, Dr. Samuel Johnson, Peter Tchaikovsky, Alexis de Tocqueville, Soren Kierkegaard, Karl Barth, Edmund Burke, Albert Schweitzer, Leo Tolstoy, Teilhard de Chardin, G. K. Chesterton, C. S. Lewis, T. S. Eliot, and, possibly the greatest scientist of all, Sir Isaac Newton, who, cantankerous as he became, rejected the Anglican church but continued to be a believer. As for Augustine, he is described in a recent biography as possessing the most titanic intellect in Western history (*Augustine — His Thought in Context*, p. 7).

Dr. Francis Collins, one of the two scientists to produce the recent break-through deciphering of the human genetic code, described himself as a Christian and at a White House presentation said that working on the project filled him with awe as it revealed something only God knew before (NYT 6/27/00).

Let us bear in mind that God is infinitely wise and ever-present, knowing the needs — not just the demands — of each of us; that he always gets his priorities straight, AND that he knows what lies ahead of each of us in any course of action we choose to take. Then, too, God is holy; he will always direct us into ways that are righteous, leading us toward a likeness of Christ — always the right relationship with God, always the right relationship with other people. This is what Jesus called life to the full (John 10:10).

This life to the full is the kingdom of God – here and now, not just in the after life. It has nothing to do with wealth or health or age, at least not directly. It involves surrender to God's will, surrender to an infinitely wiser and better source that loves us as individuals and wants the best for us as only he is in a position to know. This clear superiority of God's will for each individual is at the core of everything Jesus teaches us. I'll look more at this superiority under the heading "God's Will" in the next chapter.

The reader would do well to pause here and think this through before proceeding.

I have struggled with the question of how we live exclusively by the will of God; how do we know his will? I found that Jesus is the answer to both questions. He came and walked among us as God incarnate to die for our sins, and also to teach us about what God is like and how he wants us to live.

I found that reading the Gospel accounts in the Bible provides a solid foundation of knowledge — reading them, not just once, but repeatedly so that they become a part of me. Reading the other books of the Bible widens my perspective. Intimate, meditative prayer provides counseling and strength.

It quickly became clear, however, that I could

not do any of this fruitfully on my own. Certainly, on my own I could not give up what instinct tells me is best for me. On my own, "What's in it for me?" and "I did it my way" are powerful. Stronger than reasoning, they become ingrained habits. Reason becomes unreasonable.

Jesus is the authority and the answer. He makes it possible for all who put their trust in him to live as he taught us. We need, therefore, to know more about Jesus and what he taught — and for what he surrendered himself to death on the cross.

How to Find the Kingdom of God

A central part of the teaching of Jesus is that finding the kingdom of God is the single overwhelming need in this life. Reading the Gospels I have been struck by the importance, the extent of highest priority, Jesus placed on how we spend eternity (forever) in contrast to how we live (without him) for the moment — on taking God, his word and his will, with utmost seriousness; for example, "What good will it be for a man if he gains the whole world, yet forfeits his soul?" (Matthew 16:26).

Barclay put it mildly when he wrote that we would see life more clearly of if we looked at all things in the light of eternity (commentary on Mark 8:38-9:1).

Why ever else would God have sent his only son to come and teach us and die on the cross for us other than for the overwhelming importance that we learn to want to live by his will? The Bible teaches that those who ignore the cross, that most startling sacrifice, must explain why on judgment day — and explain it to the one who died on the cross for us (Matthew 25:45-46 and Philippians 3:18-19).

During his Sermon on the Mount (to be enlarged on later), Jesus admonished his listeners time and again not to worry, not to be anxious — for example, when he said, "Who of you by worrying can add a single hour to his life?" (Matthew 6:27) and,

So do not worry, saying what shall we wear? . . . your heavenly Father knows that you need [these things]. But seek first the kingdom and his righteousness, and all these things will be given to you as well (Matthew 6:31-33). And,

Not everyone who says to me Lord, Lord, will enter the kingdom of heaven, but only he who does the will of my father who is in heaven (Matthew 7:21).

I mentioned the use by Jesus of parables in making some of his telling points in the previous chapter. Two of his parables on the overwhelming importance of seeking and finding the kingdom of God will serve to illustrate.

The kingdom of heaven is like treasure hidden in a field. When a man found it, he hid it again, and then in his joy went and sold all he had and bought that field. Again, the kingdom of heaven is like a merchant looking for fine pearls. When he found one of great value, he went away and sold everything he had and bought it (Matthew 13:44-46).

Much has been written about every possibility of

what Jesus meant in these few sentences. But it seems straight forward. His listeners could appreciate that when you find the kingdom of heaven no cost is too great to be a part of it.

Jesus enlarged on the kingdom of heaven throughout his ministry. Everything he said and is available to us through the Gospels warrants close study and thought. He did not waste words. He was aware that his time was limited, that his purpose was nothing less than to change the relationship of the human race with God, to spread his Gospel (good news) to all nations, not just to a chosen nation, and that this would arouse deadly enmity on the part of those eager to keep everything as it was.

Some respected theologians classify the ministry of Jesus as evolutionary, as opposed to revolutionary. They argue that many things he taught had already been taught by one or another of the more enlightened rabbis at one time or another or by one or another of the great prophets. And, after all, Jesus stated clearly that he had not come to destroy one word of the Law as handed down by God to Moses.

But Jesus fulfilled the law. He taught that we should love God and our neighbor, not because it's a law, but because such love comes from the heart.

Pastor Larry Ogden has told the parable of a young woman who married an older man. Her husband made a list of each chore the wife was to perform to his satisfaction each day. He nailed it to a door so she could never forget the chores, and she dutifully obeyed. The husband died and the wife, with a sigh of relief, took the list from the door and

What Jesus Taught

put it out of sight and mind. Later, she married a young man with whom she was deeply in love. Long afterward, in search for something she needed, she came upon the list of chores her first husband had nailed to the door. Looking it over, she found to her surprise that without a thought of anything other than her desire to please the husband she loved, she was actually doing for him each day everything on the forgotten list.

> One act that from a thankful heart proceeds
> Excels ten thousand mercenary deeds.
> — *William Cowper.*

Evolutionary or revolutionary? Let the reader judge. The question is one of the trees; it is not the forest; it is a small detail not to be confused with the whole. Those who listened to Jesus seem to have found his teaching revolutionary.

A changed relationship between God and man – as presented in the Old and the New Testament — seems clear. One way to emphasize this is a cursory comparison between the concepts of God demonstrated by Jesus and by King David.

One can read into those psalms written by David that he, indeed, loved God and had faith that God loved him. Yet, he often called on God to strike down his enemies with no limits on the type or extent of ruthless violence against them, their wives and children. Also, David, who had concubines and wives, committed adultery, had the husband of his new love killed and appeared not to have realized he had sinned until God's appointed prophet told him under authority from God. True, David's repentance was great. His faith was powerful, exceptionally so. His love was far from selfless. Yet, David found favor in the eyes of God.

Jesus, who knew the Old Testament intimately, was aware of all this. Yet he taught us to live quite differently. And Jesus is the one in whom "the Father finds delight." Jesus taught and lived an utterly selfless and unconditional love. He brought to us the concept of God as Father to the individual believer.

Do I infer from this that God changed? No, God did not and never does change. It might be said that we finally reached a stage where God, in his continued unveiling of himself, saw us — at least some of us – as ready to have the sternness of his law replaced by love, a new covenant ("testament") with us brought about through Christ and the cross. How we react to that, through faith, rather than obedience to the Law, determines our relationship with God and how we shall ultimately be judged.

Two comments on the character and style with which Jesus taught. He taught straight, never pretending that his way would be easy. He was not one for euphemisms. With a startling economy of words he made profound statements that would require much thought and that would not be easily forgotten. He did not speak with nervous energy, but with the calm assurance that he was revealing truth.

All agree, Jesus spoke with authority. Whereas even the most learned rabbis began their statements

What Jesus Taught

with, "It is written that," and even prophets of old began with, "And the Lord has spoken to me that . . .," Jesus rarely cited any other authority, usually saying, "I tell you." This astonished his listeners.

There will be more on the Kingdom of God in the next chapter.

Sermon on the Mount

A working summary of the essence of what Jesus taught and how he spoke is in the Sermon on the Mount (Matthew 5-7). Here one will find the principles and rules of the kingdom.

— You have heard it said, "Love your neighbor and hate your enemy." But I tell you: Love your enemies and pray for those who persecute you, that you may be sons of your Father in heaven.

Jesus was against ostentatious religion, relegating it to the hypocrites. He taught to give and pray privately, in secret:

— and when you pray, go into your room, close the door and pray to your Father, who is unseen . . . And do not keep on babbling . . . for your Father knows what you need before you ask him.

— But if you do not forgive men their sins, your Father will not forgive your sins.

— For where you treasure is, there your heart will be also. . . . You cannot serve both God and money.

— Do not judge, or you too will be judged.

— Ask and it will be given to you; seek and you will find; knock and the door will be opened to you. . . . to him who knocks, the door will be opened.

[Barclay and others have pointed out that in the original Greek the progressive tense is used here, for example, to keep on knocking.]

— So in everything, do to others what you would have them do to you, for this sums up the Law and the Prophets.

— Watch out for false prophets.

From his elaboration on this terse warning about false prophets, it is clear that Jesus is alerting us to beware of those churches, priests, pastors and evangelists that distort his Gospel.

The Sermon on the Mount concludes with a parable about a wise man who built his house on rock, in contrast to the foolish man who built his house on sand; when the winter rains and storms came, the dry gullies were filled with torrents of surging water, the house on the sand fell, but the house on a rock foundation stood fast. Those who

What Jesus Taught

---

hear or read his words and put them into practice, he said, are like the man with a rock foundation — safe.

The point is clear: obedience to the teaching of Jesus (the will of God) is the way to life to the full.

Elsewhere Jesus cited the two most important commandments. (Given in Mark 12:30-31). "Love the Lord with all your heart and with all your soul and with all your mind and with all your strength. Love your neighbor as your self." To the first of these, which otherwise was a part of the Law, Jesus added, "and with all your mind."

I pondered what Jesus meant when he said we are to love our neighbor as we love ourselves. He surely meant more than the family next door; he meant we are to love everyone, even our enemies. In his parable of the Good Samaritan (Luke 10:30-37) he made this clear, particularly when we take into account that the Jews (his listeners) had always looked with special disdain on all Samaritans. This parable is paraphrased below. (Note the economy of words and how tellingly the parable makes its point.)

A man was going down from Jerusalem to Jericho, when he fell into the hands of robbers. They stripped him of his clothes, beat him and went away, leaving him half dead.

A priest happened to be going down the same road and, when he saw the man, passed by on the other side. So, too, a Levite, when he came to the place and saw him, he passed by on the other side. But a Samaritan, as he traveled, came where the man was; and when he saw him, he took pity on him. He went to him and bandaged his wounds. Then he put the man on his own donkey, took him to an inn and took care of him. The next day he took out two silver coins and gave them to the innkeeper. "Look after him," he said, "and when I return, I will reimburse you for any extra expense you may have."

Jesus then asked his listeners which of the three men had been a good neighbor.

The Hard Saying

Jesus said many other things, as recorded for us in the four Gospels — all important. One must read the Gospels for a good knowledge of his teaching. They richly repay careful reading. Each statement is part of a whole. To the direct quotes cited above, which are given as representative, I feel I should mention a particularly hard saying. The reader may have thought, perhaps, that loving our enemy was hard enough. It is, and no one can observe all that Jesus taught on his or her own.

The hard saying I have in mind strikes at the key to the full riches of the Christian life. The verses involved are repeated with only slight variations in each Gospel.

"If anyone would come after me, he must deny himself and take up his cross and follow me. For whoever wants to save his life will lose it, but whoever loses his life for me will find it" (Matthew 16:24-25).

Jesus never tried to cajole or lure his listeners by watered-down demands. He never pretended that his way would be easy. He may be counted on to lay it on the line. He wanted to save lost souls. He said, — and how precious this is — "It is not the healthy who need a doctor, but the sick . . . . For I have not come to call the righteous, but sinners" (Matthew 9:12-13).

Jesus knew that sinners could not be saved by what Martin Luther, John Wesley and, much later, C. S. Lewis so disdainfully called watered-down religion. True religion, as Jesus taught it, makes clear that goodness and good deeds with or without regular attendance at church cannot save souls or yield life to the full.

What did Jesus mean by the hard saying quoted above? To be a follower of Christ, to be one of his people, we need to deny self — self-will and self-trust, attempts by self to be saved. To live life to the full now and with Christ eternally we need to turn loose of self, put all our trust in him and live exclusively by God's infinitely superior will for us, not by our own flawed will.

We know our own desires, often without effort to think through the consequences; God knows what each one of us needs for life to the full now and with Christ eternally. The great part of all this is that if we confess our weaknesses and ask God to help us, Christ in us (the Holy Spirit) will see us through.

What about "take up his cross?" Jesus did not mean that we must all be crucified. We must be willing, whatever it takes, to follow the teaching of Jesus, to say no to self and yes to God. This is not to live a drab and gloomy life. There will be sacrifice, or so it may seem at first glance, serving Christ. But we are not asked to go out and seek sacrifice — just to be true to Christ in all we do. He will lead the way.

Martin Luther suggested that, if we think that living the life that Christ taught is drab and gloomy, have a look at what harlots, knaves and murderers suffer in comparison with a pious, quiet townsman or peasant. Some few have expressed a view that Christians fear death more than others. How could this be? Surely to be loved eternally and to know that this is so is the one recipe for total peace of mind.

Our task includes to love and want the best for others, and we surely need Christ's help in that. Going to a ball game or a movie may seem more fulfilling than helping someone in need, but in fact there IS more satisfaction in giving than in receiving. We don't earn forgiveness of sins with suffering. Jesus, alone, could do that, and he did it for us.

Each sentence in the hard saying quoted above fits into the next: deny yourself, pick up your cross and lose your life in order to save it. On the last point, Barclay wrote in his commentary on Matthew 16:24-26 that if we focus on being always safe, on security and comfort, we miss making life worthwhile.

And missing, one could add, the radiance of Christ's way. If we want to save — to hold on to — the self-centered life, we lose any meaning of life to the full, as well as eternity with Christ. But if we throw off the self in life and live as Jesus taught, we find the riches of the Christian life now and eternally with Christ.

I will briefly come back to this point under the heading "God's Will" in the next chapter. I'm sorry for the temporary break, but I believe there are other considerations to take into account before getting on with this. It will be helpful if readers keep in mind the hard saying quoted here.

Conclusion

Jesus knew — and knows — how hard it is to defeat powerful instincts, given the free will with which we are born. He knew — and knows — we can never do it on our own. But we don't have to go it alone. He is willing to be with us and to walk every step of the way and to be there at the end to meet us. Thus Jesus said,

"Come to me all you who are weary and burdened, and I will give you rest. Take my yoke upon you and learn from me, for I am gentle and humble in heart, and you will find rest for your souls. For my yoke is easy and my burden is light" (Matthew 11:28-30).

But, how can we come to him and how can he enable us to follow his teaching? This will be examined in the following chapter.

CHAPTER VIII

The Follow Through

❦

Christian life begins at the cross. No other event in history approaches the cross and the resurrection in profound and everlasting importance. It's worth pausing to consider why this is so.

One point can be put aside quickly. Subconsciously or not, we think of God as though he were human. Thus we ask, "How could God be one God in three persons? How could God have walked among us and died on the cross while remaining in his usual place or places doing all he usually does?"

God is spirit; he is supernatural, not subject to human limitations. He is all places at all times; he can do whatever he wants to do. His power and wisdom are infinite; it is ours that are finite.

To take another step, note God's statement in Isaiah 55:9.

> As the heavens are higher than the earth,

so are my ways higher than your ways,
and my thoughts than your thoughts.

Who among us has infinite wisdom, power, love, holiness, purity?

Sin: Consequences and Release

Being in his very nature holiness and love, God has always hated one thing: sin. Sin inevitably hurts the sinner and those sinned against; it is the opposite of love. God wants the message to be clear: love and help one another. "For the wages of sin is death, but the gift of God is eternal life in Christ Jesus our Lord" (Romans 6:23).

Throughout the Bible we humans are seen as too weak to cope with free will, as unable to live God's way, too bent on living our way. God through the cross provides the only remedy to this human predicament.

Looking back on my life, I'm amazed at my former willingness to deny any sins. Like many others to whom I have unsuccessfully witnessed for Jesus, I assured myself that, "I'm a good parent, a good spouse; I help other people in need; I'm good and kind," I insisted. Objective thought dispelled this self-reassurance, the kind of objective thought that all too often comes around two o' clock in the morning. And I came to realize that goodness of itself, no matter how good, how constant will never cleanse us of sins, never bring Christ into us.

Another defense one hears is, "I know I'm a

The Follow Through

better person than some professed Christians I've seen." This may be true, but it's irrelevant. Christ, when he indwells us, takes us as we are, and some of us are wretched, ill-tempered persons when he comes. Indeed, no one can sink too low for him.

With faith in the efficacy of his shed blood and repentance at heart we call on him; he comes. He starts — sometimes dramatically, often just quietly — the miraculous process of changing us from what we were. The Christian life is a growing process, sometimes a long process. But through it all we feel the attachment to Jesus and to his teaching and what he did for us and will yet do.

Salvation cannot begin, however, until we face up to our sins and to our inability to cope with them on our own. But take heart! I found, as readers will find, that the indwelling Holy Spirit may be counted upon to convict us of our sins and help us overcome them.

And we are not to look to safety in numbers — the "everybody does it" justification. Jesus warned against staying with the crowd — just being one of the gang. He taught, and I find his use of "broad" and "small" and "only a few" something of a shocker,

"Enter through the narrow gate. For wide is the gate and broad is the road that leads to destruction, and many enter through it. But small is the gate and narrow the road that leads to life, and only a few find it" (Matthew 7:13-14).

God is not only a loving, he is a perfect holy Father. As such, he knows the need to discipline his children. So it is that throughout the history of the human race God has imposed penalties for sins.

How else would we learn?

Before the cross, this discipline took the form of an elaborately detailed structure of ceremonial cleansing and the sacrifice of prized animals of the sinner. The way this was done, the time and place at which it could be done and the chain of priests leading to the highest priest, is in the main set forth in the Old Testament book of Leviticus, chapter 16. The New Testament book of Hebrews, a letter written to other Hebrews by an anonymous Hebrew proclaiming that Jesus is the Christ, contains an excellent summary of these ceremonial sacrifices, especially in chapter nine. Professor Barclay elaborates on this chapter with his keen historical eye and detailed knowledge of biblical times. God has made it clear that sin cannot and will not be forgiven in the absence of shed blood. We have no alternative but to accept this. It is his way.

This means of pardon for the penitent sinner was changed dramatically by Jesus when he allowed himself to be crucified, shedding HIS blood on the cross. For those who through faith accept the efficacy of that shed blood, sins are forgiven by the grace of God. They never happened. All guilt is forever removed. We must, of course, ask for that forgiveness in Jesus' name and in sorrow and wish never to sin again.

Joseph Scriven captured something of this gift of the cross in a familiar hymn:

> What a Friend we have in Jesus,
> All our sins and griefs to bear!

The Follow Through

> What a privilege to carry
> Everything to God in prayer!
>
> Oh, what peace we often forfeit,
> Oh, what needless pain we bear,
> All because we do not carry
> Ev'ry thing to God in prayer

The above diversion from the principal purposes of this chapter is to establish that (a) God hates sin and it is impossible for anyone to be saved without God's forgiveness of sins; (b) such forgiveness is always available by the grace of God, but only through penitence, faith in the shed blood of Jesus and prayer in his name. The shed blood has ever been the case; it is the case today. "Without the shedding of blood there is no forgiveness" (Hebrews 9:22).

The Role of the Cross

This brings us back to the cross. In an unprecedented moment of history God invaded time, having himself — in the form of his Son — born to a carefully selected young woman (really a girl and of no special social standing). Remember, God can do anything he wants. He proceeded, as Jesus of Nazareth, to teach us and, by living the perfect life in ordinary circumstances, to show us what God is like, how he wants us to live and why.

I would note again in passing that from this single event much is revealed about God; for example, it reveals that he is holy (his teaching) and that he is love and full of grace (his coming). How else could he have put himself through crucifixion and have asked from the cross that God forgive his persecutors" (Luke 23:34)?

God's invasion of time reached its climax with Christ on the cross, crucified, shedding his divine-human blood and dying for the sins of man. The future would never be the same.

The cross is a picture of man at his most sinful facing the unconditional love and the grace of God.

Why end the incarnate God's walk among us in this way, a way that brought to him pain and suffering beyond our imagination? It was a moment foreseen by God and predicted through his prophets from the first to the last of the Bible. It was God's way, long planned. And remember the resurrection.

It was the giant leap. The spilled blood of prized animals with its rigid ceremony and timing had brought the Israelites as far as it could. And they were adding their own human thoughts to complicate and enlarge on what constitutes sin. The cross changed dramatically the means available for the atonement of sin. It also extended and greatly intensified access to the full grace of God beyond his chosen people to all people who accept him.

The phenomenon of the cross almost defies human understanding; yet it emphasizes the unconditional love of God for us. It was a case of God at great cost obeying the will of God. For Father and Son are both God. The Father willed; the Son obeyed irrespective of the cost.

Jesus often repeated our need to obey the will of

The Follow Through

God. He lived as he taught others to live.

God is still the just Father who accepts the responsibility of teaching the deadly seriousness of sin and sins. At the cross, Jesus, knowing the will of the Father, surrendered to death by crucifixion, shedding his blood as the final sacrificial blood atonement for our sins. (It is thus that he is sometimes referred to as "Lamb of God.") He paid the price, which he sometimes referred to as a ransom, for us. Ours is to accept it for what it is and to live accordingly.

In so doing, and by the grace of God, Jesus provided to those who put their faith in him and in the efficacy of the cross, direct access to the grace of God through prayer in Jesus' name. No longer necessary are the sacrifice of prized animals, intercession by a chain of priests, special ceremonies at given times and places. In the name of Jesus we are enabled to come before the grace of God in prayer at any time, as often as we choose and wherever we may be. And there, through the shed blood on the cross, the penitent believer confessing his/her sins will be purified of all unrighteousness. It is thus that Jesus washed our sins white as snow.

> Jesus paid it all;
> All to Him I owe,
> Sin had left a crimson stain;
> He washed it white as snow.
> — *Elvina Hill*

How can this be? How could the blood shed by anyone some two thousand years ago wash our sins (present and past) so completely away that they never happened? This is a fundamental truth in Christianity. It needs to be understood without doubt. It is a precious privilege.

For starters, it's not just any man that it depends on. It depends on Jesus of Nazareth, God in the form of the Son. To this can be added that it's true because the Bible says it's so, repeatedly, with emphasis. Finally, look at all the people all through this two thousand years who have found life through this process of purification. It's true!

And we need forgiveness of sin. For while Christ on the cross gives us the opportunity, if we but take it, to be cleansed at once of all sin and guilt, we need to seek forgiveness of fresh sins each time they occur and we need help in overcoming them by the grace of God — all through prayer in Jesus' name.

The first passages in the book of Hebrews provide a fitting end to what has been written above:

> In the past God spoke to our forefathers through the prophets. . . . but in these last days he has spoken to us by his Son, whom he appointed heir of all things, and through whom he made the universe. The Son is the radiance of God's glory and the exact representative of his being . . he . . . provided purification for sins. . .
> (Hebrews 1:1-3).

The Follow Through

Our Response

Ours is the opportunity to accept the grace of God, and to grow in it. We need a change of mind with regard to sin, to God and to ourselves. This is called repentance. We must put all our trust in Jesus; go mentally to the cross; acknowledge our sins and express penitence; accept and be duly grateful to Jesus that he paid for our sins with his blood on the cross; ask and be redeemed. It's an individual thing. Jesus died for each of us — you, me.

The hymn, "Just As I Am," with which Billy Graham concludes his services, accurately summarizes the theology of redemption (free completely of past sin and guilt):

> Just as I am, without one plea
> But that thy blood was shed for me,
> And that thou bidd'st me come to Thee,
>
> Just as I am, and waiting not
> to rid my soul of one dark blot,
> to Thee whose blood can cleanse each spot,
>
> O Lamb of God, I come! I come!
> — *Charlotte Elliott*

For those to whom the passages quoted seem just too emotional, too poetic, please bear in mind that they were written by people overwhelmed by a profound reaction to what was done for them by Christ on the cross. Over two hundred years ago, and true to its title, Augustus Toplady wrote the words to a hymn still sung in most churches, "Rock of Ages."

> Could my tears forever flow,
> Could my zeal no languor know,
> These for sin could not atone;
> Thou must save, and thou alone.
> In my hands no price I bring;
> Simply to thy cross I cling.

Going back even further in time to one of Charles Wesley's hymns.

> This, only this, is all my plea,
> I the chief of sinners am,
> But Jesus died for me.

Note common threads through each of the quotations just given: humility, penitence and, above all, faith.

And it is instructive to note that John Wesley felt this after a life given to evangelical work bringing Christ to the multitudes. He preached a bold theology of Christian Perfection. Such preaching led to parting from the Church of England, so that he had to go into the open fields where he preached salvation to large crowds of common workers from coal mines and such, people who did not feel welcome in the church of their time but found deep attraction to the words that Wesley shouted to them in open fields

The Follow Through

(he was blessed with a carrying voice).

Wesley never ceased reaching out to bring others to Christ. Yet, near death, though he had never — but never — shunned works, he looked to faith, not works, for the salvation he was sure of. It was after salvation through faith that he was led to the works that God had planned in advance that he do (Ephesians 2:8-10, verses expanded on in the section below on Salvation).

We cannot on our own stay always free of fresh sins and guilt. Christ, when he walked among us, reminded his disciples that even after bathing, their feet required washing again (baths were in public places and the dust on the way home penetrated sandals). Dr. Scofield, in a footnote to John 13:10, has explained that Jesus was making the point that, while redemption cleanses thoroughly, subsequent sins need to be confessed to the Father, asking forgiveness by grace, through faith and in Jesus' name.

And it's best done promptly, so that our relationship with God remains unbroken. This is the meaning of what the Apostle John called walking in the light. It will be treated under the heading, *Salvation*.

The grace of God is essential to all — indeed, embrace it or ignore it we are totally dependent on God's grace — a grace that we do well never to take lightly or carelessly. For the forgiveness of sins, faith, penitence and a strong wish not to repeat our sins are required.

Born Again

But we cannot live Christ's way on our own. The good news is that we're not expected to. To make our efforts effective we must have Christ in us. Born with a willful nature, we must become new creations. God in his infinite mercy has provided the way. It is the new birth, a process of being born again. The very words and the concept they stand for had been neglected for too many years by too many churches. Suddenly, about the time that President Carter described himself as a born-again Christian, the concept became a catch phrase, over used and certainly not understood by those who see it as a new fad.

To Jesus the term "born again" was certainly no fad, but descriptive of a process essential in the developing life of every Christian. This had, indeed, been prophesied in the Old Testament (Ezekiel 36:26-27). Jesus told us its time had come. He said, "I tell you the truth, no one can see the kingdom of God unless he is born again" (John 3:3). It is the first step toward life to the full and eternal salvation.

As usual, Jesus did not equivocate. He didn't say that on the whole we'd be better off if we were born again. He said it was a prerequisite. He added, "no one can enter the kingdom of God unless he is born of water and the Spirit. Flesh gives birth to flesh, but the Spirit gives birth to spirit" (John 3:5-6).

The apostles of Jesus wrote of the new birth many times. God is spirit and effective prayer must be Spirit to Spirit. We must have the Holy Spirit within us.

The Follow Through

I can testify that to be born again opens to us a wonderful, uplifting and supportive life, that there is just nothing like it. Most of us are familiar with the first stanza of "O Little Town of Bethlehem." But it is in the third and fourth stanzas that the author, Phillips Brooks, gives the true message. The third is repeated below:

> How silently, how silently the wondrous Gift is given!
> So God imparts to human hearts the blessings of His heav'n.
> No ear may hear his coming; but in this world of sin,
> Where meek souls will receive Him still, the dear Christ enters in.

To be born again is not complicated. It is something Scripture promised. It is related to and for many occurs simultaneously with redemption.

We need to think long and deeply about our sins, to want to change (repentance) and to want it in earnest, to desire to become as close as possible to the likeness of Jesus. We need prayerfully to thank Jesus for dying for our (your/my) sins and to ask him to come by grace into our life as Lord, Master and Savior, and to invite the Holy Spirit by his grace to indwell us.

The Holy Spirit

When Jesus spoke (above) of the "Spirit that

gives birth to spirit," he was of course referring to the Holy Spirit, the third person of the Holy Trinity that is God. We know less about the Holy Spirit than of the Father and the Son, but we know all that we need to know. After a few missteps, I have come to feel the presence of the Holy Spirit within me almost constantly. I speak silent prayers to him frequently, most often words of praise to God, "Your will and your way." I find inexpressible comfort in this.

The Holy Spirit, when he indwells us, becomes our counselor (Jesus' word). He supplants — or builds on — our natural conscience. Through him we come to know God in ways otherwise impossible. He lets us know in unmistakable ways when we sin. By him, in Jesus' name, we come before the Father in prayer; he's the line of communication — Spirit to Spirit.

The Apostle Paul wrote that when he was especially troubled and at a loss as to how to express himself in prayer the Spirit intercedes for him (Romans 8:26). He also spoke of the Holy Spirit as a "deposit, guaranteeing what is to come" (II Corinthians 5:5). God is spirit; we are not. We must have the indwelling Holy Spirit for effective communication — two-way — with the Father.

A real problem for most of us is that all this is just too good to be true. So it is, in human terms. Bear in mind that we are coming before the supernatural. God can do anything he wants and he said he would do this. As Jesus said, "Ask and it will be given to you; seek and you will find; knock and the door will be opened to you" (Matthew 7:7).

The Follow Through

It is said that Martin Luther was in the habit of frequently interrupting his speaking on the new birth by just asking the listener to trust one who tried it and experienced it. For it is true; it has happened to countless persons. If we want it profoundly, it will be given to us by grace through faith. Count on it.

We may, when born again, actually feel the sensation inside of us, say, like streams of warm water around the area of the heart. We may simply rely on faith that it has happened. We may have no sensation at all. If we have prayerfully asked for the new birth, we should accept that it has been given to us; thank Christ and in prayer ask him to guide us.

Martin Luther's approach seems sound: even if our faith is yet weak, it completely and instantly justifies us in the eyes of God as long as the commitment on the part of the sinner ties him/her to Christ. He went so far as to suggest that to doubt salvation through justification is an insult to Christ. (The precious gift of justification is put into context below.)

When we are born again, it is not only the Holy Spirit that indwells us; Christ is also in us. In the opening passages of John, chapter fifteen, Jesus says, "Remain in me, and I will remain in you . . . . I am the vine; you are the branches. If a man remains in me and I in him, he will bear much fruit; apart from me you can do nothing."

In an intercessory prayer which he made at the last supper for his disciples and "for those who will believe in me through their message," Jesus prayed to the Father, "I have made you known to them, and will continue to make you known in order that the love you have for me may be in them and that I myself may be in them." (John 17:26).

Jesus spent much time preparing his disciples for his crucifixion and resurrection so that they would not be too disheartened when they saw him, whom they knew as Christ, arrested and crucified. He explained that it had to be, that Scripture must be fulfilled. He assured his disciples that after he left them the Holy Spirit would come into them. He told them,

> I will not leave you as orphans; I will come to you . . . . You will realize that I am in my Father, and you are in me, and I am in you ..." (John 14:18-20). He continued, "when he, the Spirit of truth, comes he will guide you into all truth . . . . He will bring glory to me by taking from what is mine and making it known to you
> (John 16:12-14).

This is how we come into a true relationship with Christ. It is above all a decision — a firm decision. He is willing. Are we? The tragedy is decision by default. Whether we realize it or not, the decision is made: to have a heart open to Christ; to have a heart closed to him. Blaise Pascal, seventeenth century French mathematical genius and founder of the modern theory of probability, is the author of what is known as "Pascal's wager" (*Pensees*). We all engage in it; it's inescapable. Translated, it goes like this: If you bet there is no God and win, you win nothing; if you bet God is real and win, you win everything.

Does the fact that we are indwelled simultaneously and permanently by both Christ and the Holy Spirit boggle your mind? Too much? Take heart!

The Holy Trinity

The mortal mind is not capable of fully understanding the Holy Trinity. It need not do so. If we think about it, there is much else about God we don't understand. What's he look like? Where is he? Where's Jesus? What'd he look like when he walked among us? Where is heaven? What's it like physically? How could the Holy Spirit dwell in thousands and thousands of individuals?

The list could go on and on. It's better if we just accept the riches in the mysteries of God. They are to our benefit. God thoroughly understands and loves us. This, surely, is enough. From what we have learned about God we can claim certain assurances.

— There is one God and he is in three persons: Father, Son and Holy Spirit.

All things considered, if we turn to the quotation just cited where Jesus spoke of the Spirit of truth coming and guiding us, it seems plausible to believe that Christ is in us through the Holy Spirit and that the Spirit does within us what he and Christ want in us. This is the view taught by John Wesley, for example.

— God is love and full of grace. It is thus with the one God and thus with each of his three persons, each of whom is one with the other. God is not interested so much in which of his names we address him by as he is in the heart, soul, and mind of the one addressing him.

— The best path for us is to persevere in worship of God through scripture and through prayer; at the appropriate time or times all we need to know will be given to us, often through our conscience, through what seems comfortable to us. We need to pray and proceed with confidence.

Remember that for God, the seeker of souls, not finite, but supernatural, all things are possible. Remember that Jesus said that such indwellings are given to all who prayerfully seek them. And recall Martin Luther's admonition, cited earlier, to trust those who have experienced it. It has happened to millions. Scripture promises it. We must put full faith in Jesus Christ and what he did for each one of us. Then by grace it will be given to us. Count on it.

The experience of John Wesley in starting wrong but getting it right is classic. Reared by holy parents and educated at Oxford, Wesley struggled to be born again. He went to the colony-state of Georgia as a missionary, confessing that his chief motive was the hope of saving his own soul" (*The Burning Heart*, p. 51).

The Follow Through

It was after his missionary experience (brief and rather dismal), after further desperate pursuit of the new birth by works that he realized that justifying faith was his need. At a small gathering in London, where the commentary of Luther (who had been through a similar experience) on the book of Romans was being read, Wesley felt a strange, persuasive warmth within and recognized it. God foreknew that John Wesley would become one of our greatest evangelists and gave him the dramatic evidence that he needed. But let us note that it did not come while Wesley was relying on works. In the end it was solely faith in Jesus and his shed blood that saved John Wesley. He never forgot it.

Jesus is the vital link — the very center of what every Christian seeks — to life to the full. The Holy Spirit comes into us through our faith in Jesus. We enter into prayer with the Father and, for example, receive forgiveness for sin only in Jesus' name.

Salvation

Once we have accepted and embraced by faith that Jesus' death on the cross paid for our sins, that his resurrection established that he is Lord and Savior, we have met the fundamental requirement of being born again. What is more, we are justified in the eyes of God, that is, by our faith in Jesus — and this alone – God by grace treats us as righteous (Romans 3:28). This is one of Christianity's most precious promises. The barrier of sin thus taken away, God shows grace and help; believing and penitent sinners can be assured that their sins are forgiven.

This is not to say that we shall never again sin. But we are given a strong desire to be like Jesus. And forgiveness and powerful help are at hand.

The New Testament gives us a number of prescriptions for eternal salvation, written at different times for different audiences. Faith is at the center of each one. In addition to prescriptions given by Jesus (see *What Jesus Taught,* above) there are prescriptions from the Apostles John and Paul. John wrote,

> But if we walk in the light, as he is in the light, we have fellowship with one another, and the blood of Jesus, his Son, purifies us from all sin (I John 1:7)

This emphasizes the point Jesus made when he spoke of the need even for those who had been to the public bath (redemption) to wash their feet on arriving home (forgiveness of fresh sins). And if we ask soon, our fellowship with God is unbroken.

Paul wrote, in Romans 10:9

> If you confess with your mouth, Jesus is Lord, and believe in your heart that God raised him from the dead, you will be saved.

Paul, in memorable lines, also wrote in his letter

The Follow Through

---

to the Ephesians (2:8-10)

> For it is by grace you have been saved, through faith –, and this not from yourselves, it is the gift of God — not by works, so that no one can boast. For we are God's workmanship, created in Christ Jesus to do good works, which God prepared in advance for us to do.

Here we come to one of the big surprises Christianity had for me. I had never before realized their existence before finding a church and pastor that taught the Bible. These profound and precise statements must be seen as a whole. They were shocking to me and would be to many Christians were they familiar with them. Goodness on its own — endless good works and deeds will not produce eternal salvation, or life to the full. That comes to us solely by the grace of God who accepts our faith in Christ on the cross as justification for salvation. Then Christ and the Holy Spirit direct us to the good works God wants. Good deeds are a by-product, not a way to salvation. Our part in finding salvation is faith in Christ and obedience to the will of God – Father, Son and Holy Spirit.

Paul left some heart-warming words about what happens to the spirits and bodies of those who die in Christ (presumably, those who have the Holy Spirit in them and have been maturing in response to his guidance).

He wrote in II Corinthians 5:6-8 and in Philippians 1:21-23 in effect that the Spirit of those who die in Christ never dies but passes instantly upon death of the body to be with Jesus. He does not say this exactly but by reading the two passages just cited, the message is clear. These scriptures tie in with the frequent references of Jesus to those who never die or parish, for example, John 3:16.

As for the bodies of those who die in Christ, they will rise as new bodies when Christ approaches at the time of his second, triumphant coming and join him; those in Christ still alive at the time will join those who were dead in Christ (I Thessalonians 4:16-17). And then we all stand before God's judgment and give an account of ourselves. On this last point about judgment, it is my personal view that we are saved to be with God eternally by faith but the inevitable judgment is on how many rewards, if any, we are given for the works referred to in, for example, Ephesians 2:8-10 (above). Jesus, it might be noted, often referred to rewards (for example, Matthew 5:12).

God's Will

To consider God's will requires a brief diversion from the trend of thought but it is important and, judging by my experience, most of us have serious questions concerning it.

If God so loves us, why not avoid the cross and just make us or create us obedient to him? This is a question already discussed. God gave us free will so

The Follow Through

that we may choose to return his love through Jesus Christ, and so that those who do so will be given eternal life with him.

For emphasis and for cohesion it is worth noting, first, a quick summary of the early paragraphs of the previous chapter.

Given that God is infinitely wise, that he knows what's ahead, and that he knows each of us intimately; given that God is holy and never wants from us or for us anything that is not good for us; given that God is love and, though he knows all our weaknesses, shortcomings and failures, loves us with a love that is bigger, kinder and warmer than possible for finite humans — given all this, how could we doubt that God's will for us is always infinitely better for us than our own will, flawed as is our will by lack of knowledge? Shouldn't it be a privilege, not a grudging task, to surrender and live exclusively by the will of God?

To be sure, God's sense of priorities is different from ours; we'll need to change. It's normal to resist, even to fear, change — and how we do fear it. But isn't it precisely our wrong priorities that get us into the muddle most of us have experienced and live in? C. S. Lewis suggests that we take our tangled web of toil and strife through self-will, self-centeredness, greed and the like and surrender them all at the cross.

Living The Riches of The Christian Life

When Jesus commanded that we deny self,

("Anyone who would come after me. . ." etc., quoted in the previous chapter), he gave us, it seems to me, the most difficult of all commands. Yet, I'm convinced that he attached great importance to it. This is where the riches of the Christian life come in. It did for me and life has become joy. I make no boast. This is all about God's grace.

The new birth put me on the right track in the right direction. I wanted the fullness of the Holy Spirit within me. Books I read advised not to push, just pray and have faith. I asked prayerfully for help to turn loose of my self-centered will, to live exclusively by God's will. Twice while in such prayer the Holy Spirit gave me the clear feeling of his fullness. I couldn't believe it! I asked, "Holy Spirit, are you telling me that you are in me in fullness?" His response was clear and affirmative.

The riches of the Christian life was beginning in me. As in all commands of Jesus, I sought in prayer to turn loose of self-centered self. Marked progress has been given me and, though still needing to affirm my surrender to God, to continue to say yes to his will, to my delight a true feeling of living in the riches of the Christian life is mine.

God has graciously given me a wonderful feeling of what I can only describe as implanted joy – a joy in my daily living, it can be briefly disrupted in circumstances of distress, but it quickly reasserts itself.

I believe that this is how we find and live the riches of the Christian life (alternatively, inner peace, life to the full). We try our best to surrender

The Follow Through

self; we seek God's help to live exclusively by his will; God takes over.

I found Dr. Lloyd Ogilvie particularly helpful on the gains from denying self, for example, in his book, *The Bush Is Still Burning*. In that book separate chapters are given on the impact of surrender on freedom from guilt, anxiety, humility, loneliness, boredom, insecurity and other problems we know or have known all too well.

Dr. Frank Pollard of the First Baptist Church in Jackson, Mississippi, in a televised service put our response to God's will in fewest words. While in prayer he said, "Lord, we'd all want to live your way if we just knew what you know."

There is a major question about God's will that haunts many. If God loves us, why does he allow hurricanes, tornadoes, floods, wars, cancer, and other miseries? He certainly doesn't want them. And he can do anything.

These are certainly valid and relevant questions. Somehow — and I just don't know why – they've never disturbed me. My own thinking is as follows. When God created the first man and woman, he gave them dominion over all things, to "fill the earth and subdue it" (Genesis 1:28) and equipped us with brains and intelligence to do so. Blaise Pascal wrote that man is only a reed, the weakest thing in nature, but that he is a thinking reed.

And what have we done with this brain power to exercise dominion through free will? Haven't we throughout history used much of our efforts to create increasingly effective instruments to hurt, maim, destroy and kill one another and to devote ourselves otherwise to harming "the enemy?" Yet it is God's will that we each care deeply for the well-being of every human being.

Isn't it that we have rebelled against God in the exercise of our free will, attempting to satisfy greed, pride, ambition and worse? This doesn't apply to all of us, isn't it true that it applies to more than enough of us to bring about a failed humanity, failed in the kind of dominion God wants? Thus it could be said that God exercises his will in two ways: his permissive free will which lets us live and devote our energies and geniuses to things that may lead to disaster; and his direct will which we should pray to know and obey. The latter requires at least our every effort — above all our willingness and prayers — to surrender self-centered will.

On this thorny issue, I again turned to C.S. Lewis' *The Problem of Pain* (pp. 51, 54) in which this subject is more amply treated. He suggested that we imagine what our world would be like if everyone on earth lived for ten years exclusively by the direct will of God, devoted to the well being of each other. Couldn't we conclude that if all the genius that is in and among us had been dedicated to the mutual well being of humankind all over the earth — God's direct will — we most certainly would have eliminated hunger and poverty; almost certainly prevention of cancer and many other diseases would be commonplace; and is it really beyond our genius, given a determination to do so, to learn to protect against, if not completely avoid, destructive weather, volcanoes and other natural disasters?

Thus, in my view, it is not God's will that we live with destruction and suffering: it is rebellion of humanity against the direct will of God that leads us to tolerate them.

Sir John Templeton, the American-born financier, seems to have the right sense of priorities. As reported in the *New York Times*, Sir John founded the Templeton Prize of Progress in Religion. He announced an increase in its value to more than $1 million for 1992, saying he wanted it to be more valuable than Nobel prizes for peace, science and literature because religion is more important to humanity.

Heaven/Hell

Here, for me, is another tough question: If God loves each of us so much, why would he let so many of us in the end go to eternal destruction, to Hell or whatever deprivation awaits most of us?

We don't know specific details about Heaven or Hell. What follows are my personal conclusions drawn from Scripture and from reading and listening to others more deeply schooled in such matters. The message that emerges from the Bible, especially the New Testament, is that Heaven is eternal bliss and Hell is eternal misery.

John, the Apostle closest to Jesus, wrote that what we will be has not yet been made known, but that we shall be like Jesus, for we shall see him as he is (I John 3:2). That was enough bliss for John.

Many theologians believe that the eternal misery that is Hell is total alienation from God and his influence. This would mean life without love, life in loneliness, eternally.

The good news about Heaven is that we are not expected to earn our way there, that it's not a race won by the swift, that it's not a competition at all; it's a place given by the loving grace of God to those who ask meaningfully for Jesus to come into their hearts and rule. The indwelling Holy Spirit leads us to know and embrace God's will, to love God and to be enabled to love others. This is a decision we can make; we then, as I see it, fit in with the set-apart society called Heaven.

The good news about Hell is that no one needs to go there. We have only to choose God's way and fit in with others in Heaven. Hell, I'd say, is a place for those left behind, those who of their own will ignore what Jesus taught and choose to live their way. It is a place for those who would just not fit in with the way of things in Heaven.

How could the afterlife be heavenly without a set-apart society, a society where there is simply no place for the self-centered, the greedy, the Adolf Hitlers, the bullies, cheats, killers, thieves and such?

We might look at choices (Heaven or Hell) in this simplified way. Suppose we all woke up one morning to learn that every living person on the planet —without exception— had become trustworthy, thoughtful and kind with regard to other people. Money would cease to have its previous dominant role, for pride would take a different place. There

The Follow Through

would be no more aggressiveness, including no more hard selling over the telephone, in newspapers, on TV, etc. If we needed to give a credit or debit card number we'd give it to anyone freely. We'd know that what we bought is good. And that what we needed was not much.

Does this sound heavenly? Perhaps that's pretty much what it is.

But now introduce a band of aggressive crooks, cheats, bullies and such. Our supposed heaven would be gone. Might such a possibility have occurred to God and led him to exclude from heaven types including those who rejected or ignored Jesus Christ?

We might ponder this proposition: death is definitive; eternity is forever; why not choose now?

Out of his love God cares deeply — witness the cross — that each one of us has every opportunity down to our last breath, of our own will, to come to him through Jesus Christ. Jesus came and told us, "No one comes to the Father except through me " (John 14:6). It's in the Bible, available to all.

After the New Birth

I used to think I could worship on my own, say a quick "asking" prayer before sleep. In fact I was self centered and that was far from enough. Once in a church that teaches the Bible, I learned that public worship supports growth in God's ways. Indeed, it is normal for the born-again Christian to want to go to church and Sunday School, to become involved. We need it.

It's a good idea to probe with care to find a church and pastor where Christ and his teaching are preached true to the whole way Jesus taught. Thus we avoid watered-down versions of the Gospel that leave one lukewarm in love for Christ. And we must shun churches that preach salvation solely through goodness and works.

Jesus repeatedly warned us against false prophets (preachers) who would come after him and attempt to distort what he had said and what he did for us. It began almost at once; it has been going on ever since. More sensationally, we read and hear of a few of the television evangelists of today who are revealed as false. The only thing new about this is television and its capacity to attract public attention. There have always been rotten apples in the barrel. And, let us note, there are many other television evangelists who do great work in bringing the true gospel of Jesus into our homes.

Even worse, in my view, are those churches – sometimes mainline churches with the largest congregations — that preach watered-down religion. If we are going to worship, it is vital to get it right. Pastors and priests provide inspiration. They are needed. The only true source of the Gospel of Jesus Christ, however, is the Bible, essentially its New Testament. We need to read it, reread and reread it; to study it on our own.

Without a personal foundation in the real and true account of what was said and what happened, we are helplessly in the hands of the pastor or priest

The Follow Through

of any church we attend. They are human, subject to human error and too often taught to preach what they believe we want to hear, as opposed to what we need. There is just no room on that narrow road that leads to the small gate, no room for watered-down religion, for luke-warm followers of Christ.

Much confusion — indeed, a veritable smoke screen — can obscure the true Gospel when false prophets take statements in the Bible out of context, in isolation or ignore them. Take, as one significant example, the words "believes in" of John 3:16: "For God so loved the world that he gave his one and only son, that whoever believes in him shall not perish but have eternal life."

Just taking this one sentence out of the context of the New Testament as a whole or, what is more, out of John's own full contribution to it, we see the need to fit such statements into the whole. The familiar sentence just repeated is certainly not saying that whoever accepts that Jesus is Lord as an intellectual fact — as merely information added to our stock of knowledge — is saved. For if we seriously accepted that Jesus is Lord, that he is the Son of God, wouldn't we spare no effort to learn all we could about the person who is Lord, and to follow his teaching.

Once we do, we learn that in the time of Jesus the words "believes in" were used with greater attention to response than now. They meant to become a follower of and committed to, putting all trust in the person in whom one believes.

With his customary bluntness, John, in his first

epistle also wrote, "The man who says, 'I know him,' but does not do what he commands is a liar, and the truth is not in him" (I John 2:4). His contemporaries would have seen John's two statements ("For God so loved the world. . .") as self-reinforcing.

Martin Luther and John Wesley are but two historically great men who felt compelled to leave the churches they had loved in order to fight against watered-down religion. Each started new movements that followed the true and full teaching of Christ and his apostles. Such painful departures have continued; even now we find some mainline churches losing out to smaller denominations that preach the Word. For it is with the true and full Word that converts to Christ feel at home.

What particularly upsets me are those churches and theologians now taking the line that we don't really know that Jesus said all of the things the Gospels have him saying. Quite a set-up: we can believe he really did say that he loves us; we can believe he really didn't say how we should respond to that love, much less the consequences of not following him. The trap is easily avoided if we just stop long enough to reason for ourselves. Here are a few salient points.

— If God created the universe and all in it, he is powerful and wise enough to do anything he wants to do. The questions, for example, of whether Jesus was of virgin birth or whether he walked on water are really questions of whether God wanted it that way. If he did,

The Follow Through

they were done

— Jesus of Nazareth is God in the person of the Son.

— God acted on a once-and-for-all basis to make the ultimate gift to mankind by sending his Son to walk among us and to show and teach us what God is actually like, how we are to live if we are to be members of his family now and for eternity. God did this knowing the horrendous cost of the cross where he took the sins of those who put their trust in him — an all-or-nothing offer to save mankind of all nations from the destruction that threatens so many. And it worked, and works, for those who respond.

— Is it conceivable that God, having planned over centuries and then done this, would watch helplessly as the image and teaching so given for posterity were hopelessly destroyed by anything less than a reliably accurate recording of what was taught, done and said?

In point of fact, Jesus foresaw the human frailty in his disciples who were to record and be the definitive sources of what he taught and did. After all, he had chosen ordinary, though deeply religious men. Increasingly toward the end of his ministry, he took them into quiet parts of the countryside and reassured them. He told them of the cross and the resurrection and warned that they, too, would be persecuted. He told them not to worry about recalling everything he had said and done. He, after his resurrection and return to spiritual form, would ask and the Father would send to them the Holy Spirit, not only to live within them, but to fill them. They would be guided by him in everything they did; all that Jesus had taught them and done in their presence would be brought back to them by the Spirit with exact clarity (John 14:26). Their speech and action tell us that this is just what happened.

The Apostle Paul wrote that, "All Scripture is God-breathed . . ." (II Timothy 3:16). Paul was well-placed to know. He had not been a follower of Jesus when he walked among us, had not heard first-hand what Jesus said. Yet he wrote much of the New Testament.

It's the way one with any faith would expect the supernatural God to work. God is not a loser. What he sets out to do, he does. Bet your life on it!

Finding the Right Way

I am persuaded that it was the Holy Spirit that in the end drove my wife and me to respond to Pastor Larry Ogden's invitation to visit his church. Not only did we there find Christ, we found Christian fellowship.

Friendships of any kind had been few and far between in my adult life. At college I had been fully occupied socially with the girl who became my wife.

The Follow Through

There had been two friends in the five years in private industry, none when farming, one, maybe two, while serving in the Navy, and none during twenty-five years as a diplomat where competitiveness prevailed.

After a week in the small church we had been led to, I had more friends than in the whole of my life before. As the church has grown, so has the number of friends. Warm friendships, sharing friendships have become a part of my life through the church. I have found that there is strength, an enriching of life, through Christian fellowship. The church that does not offer it is falling short of what is needed.

It helps enormously to read the Bible. Very early in my Christian experience I sought and received advice from Pastor Larry Ogden on which Bible was best for me. My wife and I each had family Bibles. I wanted to be sure we had the best for our purposes. We chose the New International Version (NIV). I picked up two paperback copies for my wife and me and began reading and underscoring avidly. Its riches were overwhelming. Soon after, our son and his wife presented us with a copy of the NIV as published by the New York-Oxford University Press.

The Bible by now is available in a variety of forms. The King James version has an emotional attraction for many. It is reliable. It is beautifully written in a superior literary style, in Elizabethan prose. It has been revised to eliminate archaic English usage.

The first translation of the Bible into English was that of John Wycliffe (c. 1329-1387), followed about a century later by the translation of William Tyndale (1494-1536). Both men had been outstanding theological scholars at Oxford. Each aggressively and boldly attacked the Pope of their day on a number of issues, mainly for opposition to any Bible in the vernacular that could be read by ordinary people, the laity. They made their opposition a career, knowing the risk of persecution. Their translations were printed abroad and smuggled into England and read by many. Attempts to persecute Wycliffe during his life failed. After his death his body was dug up and burned at the stake. (His enemies were sore losers.)

While Wycliffe had translated from an earlier Latin version, Tyndale made his translation directly from the original Greek and Hebrew of the Bible (one step at a time). Tyndale was imprisoned and burned at the stake.

In the eyes of many the KJV has been improved, in two ways. First, we now have a choice of reliable Bibles in contemporary language. Second, much has been learned by scholars over the centuries about the variations in meaning of words used in the languages in which the Bible was written. While more recent versions add some richness in vocabulary, they vary in no significant way from earlier versions.

The New International Version (NIV) is one of many Bibles available today. "Since 1987 it has outsold the King James Version, the best-seller for centuries . . . ." (*The Origin of the Bible,* p. 285). It is published by the New York International Bible Society.

The Follow Through

The NIV is reliable and pleasantly readable to most. It is available in paperback or about any type cover one could want. There are other versions, for example, The Revised Standard Version and the American Standard Version.

In addition, there are The Living Bible and other reliable paraphrased editions. Their readers give up some exact wording, but find an even more familiar form of presentation. It depends to some extent on whether we are by habit frequent readers. The right pastor or owner of a religious bookstore can help guide the reader to a decision. Audiotapes of the Bible are also available.

I have found that there is no substitute for reading the chosen Bible as a daily practice, a bit at a time. There's no need to start with the first page. One can start with selected parts of any of the four Gospels, for example. The Sermon on the Mount (Matthew, Chapters 5-7) is one such beginning (not the easiest). The parable of the good Samaritan and that of the prodigal son are others; they are both found in Luke (Chapter 10:30-37 and Chapter 15:11-32). Mark is the shortest of the Gospels. Matthew is essential and delightful. John is the favorite of many. Another rewarding start is to read chapters 10:1-8 and 15:1-14 of John.

My own choice of all the books in the Bible is John's Gospel. John was the disciple closest to Jesus. John emphasizes that Jesus taught the role of love. He wrote more than others of the Holy Spirit. His Gospel was written well after the others. He relates details of the Last Supper. I find him very moving.

Reliable commentaries, such as those of Professor Barclay, form useful companions and guides. The New York - Oxford University Press has published the NIV accompanied by copious footnotes and commentaries of the late Dr. Scofield.

We save ourselves much anguish when we refuse to become entangled among small details — the trees rather than the forest, or, as Aesop wrote some 2,500 years ago, "Beware that you do not lose the substance by grasping at the shadow." The four Gospels constitute a portrait rather than a biography of Jesus. There are, to be sure, variations among them. They are trifles. In the Gospels we have three different men recounting summaries of the three years they spent with their Lord. Luke, as noted earlier, is drawn from other, separate sources. Each account is valid.

It is logical that not all his disciples were with Jesus every day of his ministry. We know, for example, that Peter had a family, others may well have. Some, if not all, of them were on various occasions needed elsewhere. The Gospel of John has much material in it that the others don't. John was the closest to Jesus and his Gospel is commonly believed to have been written later than the others.

The final verse in John's Gospel sums these thoughts up in the sweeping style John sometimes used. "Jesus did many other things as well. If every one of them were written down, I suppose that even the whole world would not have room for the books that would be written"

The Follow Through

We do well to keep in mind that Jesus said, "I tell you the truth, unless you change and become like little children, you will never enter the kingdom of heaven" (Matthew 18:3).

Think for a moment of a child about four years old needing to cross a street where trucks and cars are speeding by in large numbers. The child will be frightened and in danger. Suddenly, the trusted hand of a loving parent takes the child's hand. The child crosses in comfort.

Another illustration of the kind of blind trust Jesus spoke of is in a story told by Dr. Frank Pollard in a televised sermon from the First Baptist Church in Jackson, Mississippi. I have paraphrased it below.

There were two scientists who specialized in rare birds. They heard that a pair of such birds had been seen at a certain location and rushed there to investigate. On arrival they at once sought a guide and were told of a young boy; he showed them a nest of the rare birds; it had two eggs in it. The men began offering the boy money to climb down the deep cavern and bring them one of the eggs. The boy declined. Larger and larger sums of money along with rope to secure the boy were offered. The boy finally told them, "You don't understand. I'll do it free if you'll let my Daddy hold the rope."

The true Christian needs this kind of blind trust in Jesus. It does not come from logic; it comes from knowing him, loving him — worshipping him. Reading the Bible promotes this, especially if we do not "lose the substance by grasping at the shadows." One illustration will make the point about substance over shadows.

On the evening of his arrest, trial and crucifixion Jesus was reassuring his disciples that although they would run away in fear, they would regather later. As related earlier, Peter stated flatly that he would never deny his Lord and Jesus cautioned him that before the rooster crowed that day, Peter would have denied him three times — and so, in his humanness, he did.

For years theologians most steeped in historic settings found themselves in some distress because they knew that at that time there was a law against raising fowl in the city. They concluded that Jesus had not meant literally that a rooster would crow, but that he was referring to the practice among temple guards to count their watch with the term, "a cock's crow" — a reasonable deduction, but a still more likely explanation follows.

H. V. Morton is a well-known author of travel books that blend the history of a country thoroughly into the time of writing. He was well-informed on the Bible. In his book on what was then Palestine, *In the Steps of the Master*, he wrote of being awakened early in Jerusalem by the crowing of a rooster. He inquired at his hotel if there were still laws against raising fowl in the city. He was told that there were. Morton insisted he had heard a rooster crow. He was given, with the shrug of shoulders, the answer: there always had been such laws, but the people had never obeyed them.

Along the way, often well after being born again, we find the real Christ. We experience how he deliv-

The Follow Through

ers on his offer of life to the full and leads us into the riches of the Christian life; and we'll have faith in his promise of eternal life with him. Belief in him beyond just attending church and routinely offering prayers, is what leads to a deep and meaningful relationship with him — a relationship without which we would no longer wish to exist.

We begin to understand why he makes demands that at first seem too much for us. He knows that the Holy Spirit will work in us and change what we want of ourselves. He'll do it.

It's that long narrow road to the small gate. There's less and less room for self, which only restrains his work in us. In the end — the sooner the better for us — it comes down to surrender of our will for his. The closer we become to him, the more urgently we shall want nothing less. Once our flawed self-centered will is out of his way, the sanctifying fullness of the Holy Spirit will take over. Wanting all this doesn't make it easy; instincts and ingrained habits fight back. But if we hold fast to our faith, by grace God will do what he has promised he'll do.

There are priceless messages to learn from the Christ who walked among us as though he were (temporarily) one of us. We have priceless treasures to receive from the spiritual Christ today.

That has been my experience in writing this book. I have constantly called on him and I am certain that he has been with me all the way.

Reading List

∞

Archer, Jr., Gleason L. *Encyclopedia of Bible Difficulties.* Grand Rapids: Regency Library-Zondervan, 1982.

Barclay, William. *The Daily Study Bible.* 17 vols. Philadelphia: Westminster John Knox Press, 1975-76. Used by permission.

The Life of Jesus for Everyman.. New York: Harper & Row, 1975.

Comfort, Philip Wesley, ed. *The Origin of the Bible.* Wheaton: Tyndale House, 1992.

Eusebius. *The History of the Church.* Trans. G. A. Williamson.

Bungay, Suffolk, UK: Penguin Classic Chaucer Press, 184.

Greathouse, William M. *The Fullness of the Spirit.* Kansas City: Beacon Hill Press, 1958.

Josephus, Flavius. *The Works of Flavius Josephus.* Trans. William Whiston Philadelphia: Henry

T. Coates.
Lewis, C. S. *Mere Christianity*. Barbour Publishing, Inc., Uhrichsville, OH, 1947. Used by permission.
Miracles—A Preliminary Study. New York: Macmillan, 1947.
The Problem of Pain. New York: Macmillan, 1957.
Marshall, Catherine. *Beyond Our Selves*. New York: McGraw-Hill, 1961.
Morton, H.V. *In the Steps of the Master*. London: Rich & Cown, 1934.
O' Connell, Marvin R. *Blaise Pascal – Reasons of the Heart*. Grand Rapids: Eardmans, 1997.
Ogilvie, Lloyd John. *Twelve Steps to Living without Fear*. Dallas: Word, 1987.
Outler, Albert C. *Theology in the Wesleyan Spirit*. Kansas City: Beacon Hill Press, 1975.
Pascal, Blaise. *Pensees*. London: Penguin Books, Ltd, 1966.
Plass, Ewald M. *What Luther Says—An Anthology*. 3 vols. St. Louis: Concordia.
Rosen, Moishe. *Y'shua—The Jewish Way to Say Jesus*. Chicago: Moody Press, 1982. Used by permission.
Ross, Hugh. *The Fingerprint of God*. Barbour Publishing, Inc., Uhrichsville, OH, 1981. Used by permission.
Scofield, C. I. *Oxford NIV Scofield Study Bible*. Oxford University Press, 1967.
Scott, T. Kermitt. *Augustine – His Thought in Context*. New York: Paulist Press, 1995.
Skevington, A. *The Burning Heart—John Wesley:*

Evangelist: Bethany Fellowship, 1967.

Smith, Hannah Whithall. *The Christian's Secret of a Happy Life for Today*. Old Tappan, NJ: Fleming H. Ravell.

The Christian's Secret of a Happy Life for Today. Paraphrase Catherine Jackson: World Wide Publications, 1979.

Winchester, Olive M. *The Story of the Old Testament*. Revised W. T. Purkiser. Kansas City: Beacon Hill Press,

Wills, Garry. *Saint Augustine*. New York: Penguin Putnam, 1999.

Notes on the Reading List

C. S. Lewis

C. S. Lewis was among the most learned scholars of his generation and possessed one of the great minds that have given us extensive views on religion. Fortunately for his readers his style of writing is fluid and astounding in the broadness of its sweep, the ease with which it is read and the clarity of his logic. To his very core a scholar, he read voraciously, mainly ancient literature; he taught at Oxford and eventually became Professor of Medieval and Renaissance English at Cambridge.

Agnostic throughout much of his life, Lewis reached the conclusion on a purely intellectual basis that there has to be a superior being. It was through intellectual prodding from the likes of J. R. R.

Tolkien who was to author *The Lord of the Rings* and much else, that Lewis came to accept and worship God through Jesus Christ.

Lewis' conversion was decisive. His intellect and common-sense logic permitted him to grasp the full meaning of the Bible, to speak frequently over BBC radio and to write. *Mere Christianity* is his best known book.

There is one oddity among books written *about* C. S. Lewis that deserves brief attention. Ms. Kathryn Lindskoog wrote a book published in Oregon in 1988 entitled *The C. S. Lewis Hoax*. The title rather than the content was disturbing to admirers of C. S. Lewis. The circumstance of the Lindskoog book is treated in *C. S. Lewis — A Biography* by A. N. Wilson and published by W. W. Norton, New York and London in 1990. Wilson describes the hoax book as having little to do with C. S. Lewis; that it comes down to a bitter quarrel between one disciple of the late C. S. Lewis and another.

William Barclay

William Barclay is best known in America for his books published as part of *The Daily Study Bible* series. The series consists of commentaries written by Barclay on each book of the New Testament. Barclay's American publisher puts it well in writing that his scholarship was so thorough and his style of writing so brisk that while he is instructing the reader by what he says, he is also delighting the reader by

Notes on the Reading List

the sheer charm with which he says it. His commentaries enrich the reader's understanding and appreciation of the New Testament. They reflect a lifetime of reading, studying, preaching, and teaching.

Barclay inherited from his father a passion for reading. His commentaries sparkle with events and quotations from the lives of others — great, small, famous — from all ages of history.

One quick example will make the point about enrichment by commentary. Many agree that the Gospel of John is the most profound and rewarding to the reader of all the gospels or any book in the Bible. Yet, John begins his Gospel with words that, while full of meaning, put off some readers by an apparent air of mysticism. Barclay's commentary clarifies this and brings to it the life John put into it. Thus, "In the beginning was the Word and the Word was with God, and the Word was God." Barclay reminds us that John wrote in Greek, the language understood by most readers all over the known world and certainly by the Greeks who were his immediate target. The Greek word used by John for the "Word" (Jesus) is "Logos," loosely translated into "word," but meaning so much more. What is being said, Barclay wrote, is that Jesus, later identified by John as the "Word," is none other than "God's creative and life-giving and light-giving word, that Jesus is the power of God which created the world and the reason of God which sustains the world. . . ."

Eusebius

Eusebius' *The History of the Church* covers three centuries of Christian history — in effect, what happened between events in the Bible and the arrival of a benign ruler, Constantine. After reading and studying the Bible many curious minds feel a keen urge to know what happened after the highly vulnerable church was first established. The Bible, in this respect, leaves the reader uninformed.

Drawing his information about previous generations from a remarkable number of earlier writers, most of whose writings are no longer available, Eusebius left a treasure that is irreplaceable. From him we learn, just as an example, that Peter was crucified, that Paul was publicly beheaded, and that John Mark was the first to carry the Gospel to Egypt where there were so many Jews. Eusebius' work has been published with a masterly introduction by its translator, G. A. Williamson, a British scholar who also translated an edition of Josephus' *The Jewish War.*

C. I. Scofield

Dr. Scofield, author of a number of religious books, a lecturer on such matters in the United States and Europe, Pastor in Dallas and in Massachusetts, introduced in 1909 the long-standing study method adapted now into *The Oxford NIV Scofield Study Bible*. The advantages for some of the NIV (New International Version) of the Bible are mentioned in the final chapter of this book. The combination of Dr. Scofield's commentaries (previously available in some editions of the King James Version of the Bible) with the NIV Bible brings the Bible's text in contemporary English and the Scofield aids into one book.

Dr. Scofield lived a life of amazing variations and dedication to all he did. He fought in the American Civil War under General Lee and received the Confederate Cross of Honor. He was appointed by President Grant, no less, United States Attorney for Kansas. Six years later he was converted to Christianity and, by 1882 was ordained. His commentaries and cross references reveal an exceptionally intimate knowledge of the Bible and its contents.

Hugh Ross

Dr. Ross in his book *The Fingerprint of God* writes with sure knowledge and respect for the sciences. He has a degree in science and a Ph.D. in astronomy. He was for several years a post doctoral fellow at the California Institute of Technology, where he continued research on quasars and galaxies. He is now president of *Reasons to Believe*. He lectures frequently on TV and to special groups. His book is enlightening and a pleasure to read, impressive by the ease with which he treats great questions and great scientists and the straight forwardness of his conclusions.

Lloyd John Ogilvie

Dr. Ogilvie was senior pastor of the First Presbyterian Church in Hollywood. He is more widely known for his syndicated television program, "Let God Love You." That title says much about his general approach in ministry. He is gifted with an easy writing style that makes reading him a pleasure. He has written much, with the hope of more to come. He does not present God as a Santa Clause; on the contrary, he faces frankly the task of finding life through Jesus by complete dependence on him and by daring faith (his words). This he does with joy, emphasizing the benefits. Dr. Ogilvie was chosen to serve as Chaplain of the United States Senate in January 1995. His many works include: *The Bush is Still Burning — The Christ Who Makes Things Happen in Our Deepest Needs* and *If God Cares, Why Do I Still Have Problems?*

Gleason L. Archer, Jr.

Dr. Archer, professor at Trinity Evangelical School, Deerfield, Illinois, has an impressive background. He holds a B. D. from Princeton Theological Seminary, an LL.B. from Suffolk University Law School and a Ph.D. from Harvard; he taught Arabic studies in Beirut and is the author of many books. Especially recommended for those who want their facts straight is the *Encyclopedia of Bible Difficulties*. Dr. Archer's purpose in this book is to resolve every apparent contradiction in the Bible, Old and New Testament. He argues authoritatively for the unity and the integrity — the inerrancy — of the Bible. Far from being a dry document, his book is hard to put down.

Dr. Francis Collins

Dr. Francis Collins, one of the two scientists to produce the recent break-through deciphering of the human genetic code described himself as a Christian and at a White House presentation said that working on the project filled him with awe as it revealed something only God knew before (NYT 6/27/00).

Printed in the United States
1031300001B